DEATH at the FESTIVAL

Barbara Yates Rothwell

Order this book online at www.trafford.com
or email orders@trafford.com

Most Trafford titles are also available at major online book retailers.

Print information available on the last page.

ISBN: 978-1-4907-7429-9 (sc)
ISBN: 978-1-4907-7430-5 (hc)
ISBN: 978-1-4907-7431-2 (e)

Library of Congress Control Number: 2016909044

Trafford rev.   06/06/2016

www.trafford.com

North America & international
toll-free: 1 888 232 4444 (USA & Canada)
fax: 812 355 4082

Murder is never funny, but I think most people concerned with solving such a crime would agree that some of the folks involved have their peculiar side. Some of them are in here.

This tale takes us back to the days when police had to manage without mobile phones, computers and super-sophisticated forensics. Enjoy!

IT WAS THE FIRST TIME—never killed anything before, not even a rabbit. Breathing a bit uneven, but in general pretty good. Hands steady. It was faintly surprising, looking down at the body, that there were no emotions, no rage, no satisfaction, now that this preliminary deed had been accomplished. Shock, revulsion perhaps, those had been expected—a trembling to match the awfulness of what had just occurred.

But there was nothing. Not even a sense of purging, in spite of the fact that this death was really quite symbolic.

In a way, one could be sorry for the woman who had inhabited the corpse lying on the floor. She hadn't deserved to die, and so the whole business had been kept as simple as possible, as unthreatening. There had been no wish to torment her. Her well-known smile was welcoming, the door was opened wider, and then there was a momentary look of astonishment—no, not really fear—when she had seen the gun and taken the bullet all in the same second.

She had fallen with the flowers, grabbing them instinctively; then slipped, almost elegantly, to the crimson carpet that hid bloodstains, and had lain there, surrounded by roses and carnations, her wounded face turned away as if she wished to be discreet even in this final moment.

~~~~

1

'Better than ever this year,' Sir Beverly Stainer was saying to a group of friends drinking the free champagne. 'Every year a new challenge, eh, Hogbein?'

'We aim to please,' Hogbein said, smiling. He could afford to smile now. The Festival was well into its run, and such administrative hiccups as there had been were long since soothed. Unless something totally unexpected happened—the King's Hall roof falling in or a tsunami flooding the riverside art gallery—they now seemed set for a good festival. There was a sense of gaiety, here in the luxurious basement of the Royal Hotel; the evening's concert had been a huge success, and it amazingly seemed as if they might be going to break even this year.

'What about this woman—this Camille Lag...Lag...?'

'Ligorno,' Marius Hogbein said, only a little shortly. Sir Beverly's inability to remember anything but the name of a horse was too well-known to take offence at. 'Brilliant! Did you enjoy it?'

'Pretty little thing,' Sir Beverly said, beckoning a waiter for more champagne. 'Gifted, too! Fairly raced up and down that piano. Makes you wish you'd practised more, eh?' He laughed noisily. His guests smiled appreciatively. It was worth making the effort. Sir Beverly was a very rich man. 'I suppose you like that kind of thing, Hogbein? Bach and all that?'

Hogbein nodded. '*Very* fond of Bach! An amazing composer, as fresh today as he was two and a half centuries ago.'

'Ah yes, well, you would.' Sir Beverly excused the festival director with a pitying smile. 'Your bread-and-butter, what? Couldn't have *you* going round saying you didn't like Bach, could we?' He roared again. 'Myself, I prefer *Offen*bach! Same diff, eh? Can-can, you know! Frilly skirts and all that jazz. Ought to have an Offenbach festival some time. Yes, why not? You'd get the numbers, and that's the important thing.'

Marius Hogbein smiled until his cheeks hurt, wishing as he did so that some particularly nasty thing would fall on the fat knight's head. He had inherited Sir Beverly from his predecessor, and it had been impossible to unship him from his position as chairman of the Festival.

'Certainly, numbers are important,' he said courteously. 'But not paramount.' Coral Stone, his secretary, gave him a tight, private smile from across the table and he stared back at her, trying to focus in his eyes patient humour and wry disgust. But he suspected that, half full of champagne as he was, he simply looked cross-eyed.

'What do we have to look forward to next?' Mave Cardwell said, leaning across the table towards him. Her expression said, 'let's cut this foul man out of our conversation!'

'In your line of business,' Marius said thankfully, turning towards her, 'tomorrow night's updated version of 'Pygmalion' with an all-black cast.'

Mave pulled a face. 'Oh, for an evening with the Bard in Elizabethan dress!'

'You surprise me,' Marius said. 'A drama critic looking backwards? Why am I bothering?'

Mave laughed, a rich sound full of mockery. 'You tell me, honey! What do people want? Does anyone know? *I* don't.' She turned to Hal Princeton, sitting at her side immersed in cigar smoke and gin. 'Do you know what *your* public wants?'

'Tchaikovsky, Brahms, Beethoven, and nothing after ten o'clock. At a guess.'

Alicia Hogbein regarded her husband. 'Were you happy with tonight?'

'The concert? Terrific! A lovely lady. Amazing how she gets so much power from those slim little arms and tiny hands. Must be made of steel.'

Princeton smothered a yawn, born of weariness rather than boredom. Festival time was demanding for those whose job it was to keep the public informed about what they had seen and what they should think about it.

'Shirr-strong as a horse—a lady horse, let's say. But you're right—she's lovely. Anyone who knows her will tell you. Charm, grace...' He waved his cigar perilously close to Sir Beverly's face, and the chairman leaned away pointedly. 'Sorry, ol' man...' He stood slowly, holding on to the table edge for support until he got his legs properly balanced under him. 'A lovely lady, an' I don't mind who hears me say it! Come on, ol' girl...'

He held out a hand to Mave, and she, shrugging and pursing her lips at the company, rose in more genteel fashion and gave a comprehensive wave.

''Bye, dears! See you tomorrow—somewhere.'

Marius watched her go. Alicia was collecting bag and lacy stole and making the obvious movements of departure. He sighed suddenly in spite of himself. If he woke up tomorrow and found that the rest of the Festival had been cancelled and he could do nothing about it—well...No, perhaps not! Too much work had gone into it to back out now, even in his imagination. But he couldn't altogether help looking forward to the end of the season, and three weeks in Europe being himself. With Alicia, of course. She would visit all the museums and art galleries, and he—well, he would probably visit all the museums and galleries, too. He usually did. Out of one set of bonds into another!

As he stood and made his farewells and helped Alicia into her stole he sighed again. It wasn't that he was bored. So what was it? Perhaps he was just too confoundedly efficient, he thought all at once, surprising himself. He planned everything so that there would be no problems, and then when there were none he began to wish for a judicious hiccup or two for him to deal with.

They reached the top of the velvet-draped stairs and found that the night had grown cool with the smell of rain. At least there was nothing in the open air for the next few days. Cancelling was always a hassle.

'It was a good concert,' Alicia said as they reached the car. 'She really is a splendid lady, Camille Ligorno. I'd like to have time to talk to her tomorrow.'

'So you shall. I'll get Craig to arrange it for you.'

But in the morning they found the delightful Madame Ligorno lying amid the crushed flowers in her hotel room, and nothing looked easy any more.

2

It worried Marius that his first sensation, after the first jolting shock of Madame's death, was relief that she had fulfilled all her commitments to the festival. She had arranged to have a couple of days free afterwards, an opportunity to make the most of the wide Australian beaches and perhaps even to see other distinguished performers whose paths seldom crossed her own, and so were too often no more than a name in a catalogue or pure and beautiful sounds issuing from a compact disc.

He told himself that his reactions were quite understandable; but he was relieved that his secondary emotions were less egocentric. He spoke to the police outside the door of the murder room.

'Did she...do they think...do you suppose she suffered at all?'

The policeman shook his head. 'Couldn't have. Instantaneous, the doc says.'

Marius gave a deep sigh. 'Thank God for that, anyway. A lovely woman like that—unbearable to think...'

The man nodded sympathetically. 'Makes you wonder, doesn't it?'

'I'd like to see whoever's in charge,' Marius said. 'I feel somewhat responsible.'

But it was early to know anything for sure. There was plenty of bustle in and around the room, police photographers flashing their cameras, detectives filling notebooks, and the slow movements of other guests past the door in the hopes of seeing something they could later relate, however vague. Marius went downstairs and into the coffee lounge, where several of his own staff were sitting, eyes on his as he entered, an unspoken question hanging in the air. Faces were pale under their midsummer tan, and the euphoria of the past few nights had quite disappeared.

'Anything?' Coral said quietly, and he shook his head.

'I think you should go back to the office in case people are trying to contact us.' He patted her shoulder gently. She looked haggard in the morning light. The festival press officer, Jim Fletcher, stood up and hesitated for a moment. 'Yes, Jim?'

'Do you want a press release? Is it appropriate?'

Marius frowned. 'I suppose so. I don't know. This is one thing I have no experience of. Get one ready.' He put a hand briefly on the other man's arm. 'Bring it to me and we'll see what's necessary.' He pressed his fingers into his eyes. 'I suppose there should be a formal statement from the festival, as well as all the garbage the newspapers will cough up.' He nodded encouragingly to Jim, and the young man left quickly, as if he was glad to have something constructive to do.

'My God!' said someone behind Marius, with a whoosh of sound from the automatic doors as she swept in. 'You poor old devil, Marius!' It was Mave Cardwell, of course, always at top pressure, always on the job. He turned to greet her, and was taken aback by a kind of glee in the over-powdered eyes. 'What a tragedy! What a story! This'll go round the world!'

'We could have done without it,' he said mildly enough, and she snorted back at him.

'International recognition for the festival that wiped out one of the world's greatest performers!'

Marius groaned. 'Spare me, Mave. I've got enough to worry about.'

'But she'd finished her stint for you, hadn't she? What can you lose?'

'Mave!' he said, shocked in spite of himself. 'We're talking about murder. About that 'lovely creature' we were discussing last night.' He stopped suddenly. 'At just about the time, according to the doctor. Oh, *Lord*!'

'Sit down,' she ordered. 'You need a drink. Have you had any breakfast?' He shook his head. The news had broken just as he was coming out of the shower. Alicia had told him, eyes wide and tragic. 'Then you must eat, sonny!' She called to a waiter and ordered quickly. 'Can't have you fainting on the job, old boy.'

He felt better after he had eaten. One corner of the lounge had been tacitly taken over by the festival staff and hangers-on, and they were secluded, away from the normal comings and goings. 'So what happened?' demanded Mave, watching Marius finishing his second fried egg.

'She was shot. But apart from that, I don't know. No one's told us.'

'What a wicked thing!' Mave exclaimed with an undercurrent of satisfaction. 'To bring to an end a life filled with such—such glories. Who could have done such a thing?'

'You'll have to ask them.' Marius pointed to a couple of policemen crossing the foyer. Mave looked up.

'I believe I will.' She stood and made her way with determination across the wide hall, stopping the men in their progress. They listened to her courteously enough, but Marius could see they weren't telling. He smiled wryly to himself. He liked Mave, even her shocking halo of unrealistically black hair, but there were times when her exuberance for life in all its rainbow shades got out of hand. She pulled a face at the men, expressing her frustration, and returned to the corner of the lounge.

Marius took the opportunity to excuse himself, rejecting politely Mave's offer to come with him to the office. He needed to be alone, to think. Death was one thing. It would have been bad enough to find Madame in her bed, her life ended by a heart attack. But murder implied other things, dark things that he didn't want to think about, but must. He must try to set the whole period of time since Ligorno had arrived in the city fixed in his mind, so that he would have some kind of framework for the police enquiries. Murder meant a victim; but it also meant a murderer.

Coral Stone was sitting at her desk when he entered the office. She turned to him with a question in her eyes. 'I know,' he said. 'Don't ask me anything now.' He passed through the outer room and closed the door on his own office, leaning back against it for a moment. The Festival, which had stretched before him, neatly and efficiently planned, now seemed a shambles. He remembered his discontent of the evening before, and wished it back so that he could relish the sensation of having no particular problems. Dimly he was aware that phones were ringing, but he ignored them.

Craig, the administrative officer, knocked gently and entered, his face drawn. 'Sir Beverly for you, Marius. Will you take it?' Marius started to shake his head, then stopped.

'Yes. Put it through.' He picked up the receiver. 'Sir Beverly?'

The voice at the other end of the line was harsh and angry. It seemed he might be blaming Marius for the tragedy. He simply held the phone and allowed the sound to continue. 'Well?' said the distant voice. 'What are you doing about it, eh? What are you actually *doing*?'

'We are doing whatever is necessary.' Marius's own voice was colourless. 'It's in the hands of the police. There's not a great deal we can do—except answer the phone and help in any way possible.'

Sir Beverly humphed grumpily. 'Keep me informed. I ought to be informed! See to it!" He slammed the receiver down. Marius stared into the earpiece before replacing it with commendable control.

'Three bags full, Sir Beverly!'

'Dame Clarissa for you,' Coral said, putting her head round the door; and before he had time to think what he should say the formidable lady was upon him. Tall, elegant, regal in style, she had been chairperson of the Festival Friends for ten years, and associated with the festival for thirty. He was very fond of Dame Clarissa—though he could have done without her at this moment.

'A terrible thing!' she was saying. 'Frightful! Frightful! In our festival, too. Are you all right, dear boy? You must be feeling absolutely shattered.' Dame Clarissa always spoke with a decibel range that implied that you were in a far paddock with the wind against you. It probably came of being reared on a Northern Territory cattle station before marrying the late Colonel Osbert Payne, whose main claim to fame had been his undoubted success on the parade ground of the Victoria Barracks.

In his lighter moments, Marius had sometimes wondered how their more intimate conversations would have been conducted—*molto vigoroso e sempre fortissimo,* he imagined. But she was a dear, in spite of it.

'Come in, Clarissa. Yes, it's been a sad blow.' They sat down and regarded each other silently.

'You look distinctly peaky, dear boy. Don't let it get you down. It wasn't your fault...' She stopped suddenly, and they caught in each other's faces the knowledge that this was not a matter of blame, but of criminality. Someone—and it was likely it was someone they knew—*was* responsible. 'Oh dear,' the old lady sighed, looking her years for once. 'Oh dear, dear, dear...'

'I suppose the problem is...that there's nothing we can do,' Marius said after a while. 'It's in police hands. You feel you want to go rushing round saying to people, "where were you at the time the crime was being committed?"'

'But you can't do that! I just hope they've got somebody on it who understands what they're handling. After all, it has international repercussions. She was a very great lady. Many people are going to be broken-hearted over this affair.'

'I don't think we're right to *assume,*' Dame Clarissa said slowly, 'that it *must* be someone from *here.* Couldn't it be some kind of—um—international syndicate—isn't that what they call them? Couldn't it be...ah...?'

'It could be. But let's face it, it's not very likely. The people who are involved with the festival, the people who were involved with Camille Ligorno, they're all people known to me. They're all people known to *all* of us, Clarissa! That's what makes it so devilish. But we can hope—for an outsider, someone off the street.'

Coral opened the door quietly, peeped round. Behind her was the figure of the detective in charge; Marius pushed back his chair and stood, defensively. Dame Clarissa stood, too, her eyes going from his and Coral's to the unrevealing face of the man beyond.

'You'd like me to go, dear boy!'

'No! No, Clarissa, you stay. We're all going to be in this.'

The detective entered, confident, authoritative, at ease in this room from which the ease had departed. Behind him, his young constable.

'Marius Hogbein? Nick Verdun, detective sergeant. This is detective constable Briggs.' Both men flashed their ID, and Marius nodded.

'Do sit down.'

'Sorry about the interference with your timetable, sir. But we want to get this matter wrapped up as quickly as we can.'

Marius looked as if he was going to say something, then turned, indicating Dame Clarissa, who had seated herself once more. 'May I introduce the lady who has been a close friend of the festival for many, many years...Dame Clarissa Payne.'

Dame Clarissa gave one of her most aristocratic bows, sitting upright, Queen Mary among the peasants. Verdun managed to look suitably impressed. 'Ma'am!'

'Now,' he said, 'we'd like to get as much information down on paper as possible, so that we can start planning our line of campaign.'

Marius hesitated briefly. 'Have you a clue—anything to go on?'

'Early days yet, sir,' the man said reassuringly, a bloodhound prepared to wait for ever for the right scent to materialise.

'I just wondered,' Marius said apologetically.

'Believe me, sir, we shall keep you informed. We are well aware that this is a difficult time for you—for all of you.'

Carol entered with a tray and cups of coffee and handed them around. '*Good* girl!' Marius said with greater enthusiasm than necessary. Verdun glanced up from the notebook he was opening, and Marius leaned back, closing his mouth sharply. *'Mustn't show nerves',* he told himself. *'They'll be looking out for nerves.'*

'Thank you,' Verdun said, taking his cup but putting it away from him, as if he had no time to waste. 'Now, Mr Hogbein—your full name, if you please.'

3

In the outer office there were sporadic attempts being made to work as if nothing had happened. As Coral Stone had said several times (before her eyes filled with tears and she had to leave for the ladies' room in a hurry), in every way but one this was a normal working day; and Marius would need all the help he could get.

But it wasn't that easy. Between Coral and her typewriter, between Craig and his administrative piles of paper, between Jim Fletcher and his impending press release, lay a dark area from which the beautiful eyes of Madam Ligorno stared at them woefully.

'But why Camille Ligorno?' Coral cried suddenly, pushing her chair back. 'Who would have anything against her? Was anything stolen? It's so—so personal, going to her room and shooting her, just like that. You could almost understand it if it had been out in the streets—robbery with violence or something. But this!'

Jim nodded solemnly. 'A beautiful, gifted creature like that! It doesn't seem possible.' He picked up his pen as if to work, then laid it down again. 'It doesn't seem motiveless, somehow. It seems...' He shuddered suddenly. 'It does seem too damned personal altogether. Like it might have been...' He stopped.

Coral nodded. 'One of us? Yes. That's probably what they think.' She tipped her head towards Marius's closed door. 'The police.'

'Coral Stone,' Marius was saying. 'Been with me for ten years. Divorced about six years ago. No family. Totally reliable, the heart of the festival in many ways.' He watched Verdun and Briggs making notes. 'Do you need anything more about her?'

'No. Not just now. The two young men in the office?'

'Craig Schuster. About thirty. A widower, though he doesn't talk much about himself. Scientist turned musician. Very able—splendid administrator. Gets on with everyone in a quiet, slightly reserved manner.'

'Out-of-festival interests?'

'Wouldn't have an idea,' Marius said. 'During the build-up to the festival he is totally involved—hours of overwork without complaint. But in the slack times—you'll have to ask him.'

'Women?'

Marius raised his eyebrows. 'I've never thought about it. He doesn't seem the type for a light affair, but that's only an opinion. I suppose you might say he has the air of a married man, even though he no longer has a wife.'

'And the other? Fletcher, I think.'

'Jim? In advertising. Decided he didn't like the ethical values. Or lack of! A rather moral young man, in a way. Very likeable, very trustworthy. Puts out good press releases. I believe he expects to get married in a month or two. Nice young fiancée, I'm told, works somewhere down near Bridgefield.'

'Would any of your staff have had any contact with Mme Ligorno outside the normal business of the festival?' Verdun was watching carefully. Marius tried to think. Could there have been any contact? He shook his head doubtfully.

'I think it's highly unlikely. This was the lady's first trip to Australia...'

'And her last!' Dame Clarissa said suddenly in dark-hued tones; the men, taken aback, inclined their heads in unison.

'Indeed!' Verdun said. 'It is a great tragedy.' He snapped the notebook shut and stood up. 'We shall try not to disrupt your activities too much, Mr Hogbein. But I would ask you to keep yourselves available as much as possible. One never knows when a lead may pop up.' He nodded to Marius, made a brief bow in the direction of Dame Clarissa, and was gone, the silent Briggs at his heels.

Marius stood and went to the window. He was annoyed to find that his hands were shaking. When he turned he saw that Dame Clarissa's eyes were on him with a look of intense compassion. He gave a half-smile. 'Silly, isn't it? To feel guilty about something that isn't your fault.'

She shook her head slightly. 'Quite natural. You have to have a sense of responsibility for the people who come here for the festival. So of course you feel it when something like this happens.' She was unusually gentle. 'I'm very fond of you, Marius. I never had children, you know—only the one who died in a week…damned tropical posting! But if that one had lived he would have been about your age. So I feel something…' She hesitated. 'Forgive me, dear boy! The excitement has made me maudlin.'

Marius moved slowly across the room and bent to put an arm around the old lady. Her shoulders under his hand felt unexpectedly fragile, belying the air of indomitable strength that normally surrounded her. He put his cheek against her soft, old face and for a moment they remained close, relaxed, sharing an affection which neither had admitted before. 'You have always been a great strength to me,' he said at last. 'I have been very fortunate.'

She broke the mood, straightening her back and preparing to leave. All at once she gave an undignified snort. 'I always hoped that in some way I made up for Sir Beverly!'

Marius, released, gave an explosive laugh. 'If anyone could,' he said, grinning at her, 'it's you!'

4

Coral showed the detectives into a small room and closed the door behind her. She was nervous, her hands sweaty, but she hid the signs. 'Do sit down.'

'Just a few routine questions at this point,' Verdun said. 'You can understand, we come into a case knowing nothing about the people involved, and so we have to familiarise ourselves very quickly with details which you may have had months or years to get to know.' He gave her an appreciative smile. She was a good-looking woman, and he enjoyed working with attractive people. His job too often led him to the other sort.

'I suppose you do. I hadn't thought of that.' She gave him a small, cautious grin. 'How can I help you?'

'Did you know the deceased—Madame Ligorno—apart from your festival relationship?'

'No. I hadn't actually met her until I went to the airport the other day to pick her up.'

'What was your impression of her?'

Coral stared past him. Tears were threatening at the thought that that wonderful artiste could now only be spoken of in the past tense.

'A warm, lovely person. Beautiful, really, especially when she was made up to go on the platform. A very generous sort of woman.' She hesitated. 'Sometimes you feel a kind of antagonism from these famous women, as if they suspect they are always under threat. But Madame...' She shrugged. 'I can't imagine why anyone would want to harm her in any way. She was in some way—*special!*' She saw the eyes of both detectives on her. 'Not because she's dead. I know no one wants to speak ill of the dead. But it seems to me quite incomprehensible that anyone should have wanted her killed.' She leaned forward urgently. 'Do you have *any* idea...?'

Verdun shook his head. 'Not at this stage.' He stood, indicating that the interview was over. 'May I see the two men in the office? One at a time. If you would be so good.'

While they waited, Briggs cleared his throat and said, "Excuse me, Sergeant..."

Verdun had walked to the window and was looking out at the serenity beyond: the river, sails, a small dinghy or two, and the ferry making its relaxed journey across to the far shore. 'Yes, Briggs.'

'Just wondering...what do you want me to do?'

'What you *are* doing, Briggs—watching and hopefully learning. This is your first murder, isn't it?'

'Yes.'

'So you've got a lot to learn, haven't you?'

'Yes.'

'Keep making your notes. We'll compare them when we get back to the office.'

'Sir!'

The door opened and Jim Fletcher came in with a worried frown. Verdun waved him to a chair and Jim sat, hands on knees, plainly uneasy.

'Just a few questions, Mr Fletcher.' He went through the information already given him by Marius, checking for accuracy. Then he asked the questions Coral had answered.

'No—no. I had never met the lady. Not till Coral brought her into the office the other day. Been a great fan, of course. Who hasn't?'

Nick Verdun, who had never heard of Camille Ligorno until this morning, nodded gravely.

'Your movements last night?' Verdun said suddenly, putting his head back so that he could look down his nose towards the other man. Jim blinked at him.

'Last night?'

'We estimate that the time we are investigating could not have been before eleven, when the deceased went up to her room—watched by several people in the foyer—nor after about twelve-thirty, according to the doctor's report. Where were you at that time?'

For a moment blind panic gripped Jim, and it showed in his eyes. He had heard of people being asked this question; it seemed ridiculous he could not remember anything at all about the previous evening. 'I…I—well, of course,' he said with a rush of relief, 'I was in the lounge, the hotel lounge. Most of us were.'

'All the time?' Verdun's eyes never left his face. It was eerie.

'Well, not *all* the time, I suppose. One obviously got up to—to go to the toilet, for instance. Yes, I do remember leaving the party twice…I think…' His voice trailed off. How could he prove it? Had anyone else been in the loo?

'Anything else?'

He frowned desperately. 'The phone! Somebody rang for Marius—Mr Hogbein. I took the call.

'Ah! And who was it calling?'

Jim's face fell. 'I don't know. By the time I got there the phone was dead. Cut off, perhaps. Or from a call-box—ran out of coins? Something like that.'

'A pity.' Verdun closed his notebook, still regarding Jim's flushed face with interest. 'Well, thank you. Please keep in touch.'

Jim stood quickly. 'Yes, I will—yes, I will! We shall be very busy—especially now, I suppose. A lot of loose ends…you know…' He opened the door and left, nodding back to the man whose eyes seemed calculatingly interested in him. 'Oh, my God!' he muttered to Coral as he passed her desk. 'What a ghastly mess!'

Craig Schuster stood, smoothing his hair as he hesitated briefly. Coral nodded at him. 'Your turn.' He crossed the room and knocked on the door through which Jim had just emerged. Verdun called from inside.

'Ah, Mr Schuster! Please sit down...I won't be a minute.' The detective was writing something, and Craig sat down opposite to him and regarded him curiously. Briggs was staring stolidly at him, his inexpressive gaze hiding a sudden desire for food. He wondered if there would be a lunch break; probably not, the way the sergeant was behaving. The silence became slightly oppressive. Craig shifted in his chair.

'There!' Verdun looked up, a small smile on his face. 'You're an administrator yourself, they tell me, so you'll understand how *my* administrators tick. They like everything down in black and white.' He leaned back. 'Schuster! German origins?'

'I suppose so. At some time. But my father was an American, came over here during the war and stayed.'

'Still here?'

'No. Died in the late fifties. From wounds received in the Pacific fighting, though of course no one ever admitted it.'

'Mother?'

'Australian. Died five years ago. Cancer.' He invited no further questioning. His mouth closed almost stubbornly. Verdun took notice of the fact.

'You yourself are a widower, I understand?' There was a perceptible pause.

'I am.'

'When?'

'Three years ago.' He looked directly into Verdun's face. 'Is it necessary to go into this? I find it painful.'

'My apologies, Mr Schuster. I need to know the background. Well, let's get to the matter in hand. Can you please tell me—did you know Mme Ligorno before she arrived here last week?'

'No.'

'Did you have any dealings with her outside the realms of your festival duties?' Craig shook his head firmly. 'Where were you last night between eleven and twelve-thirty?' He kept his eyes on Craig's face.

'We were all together, at the hotel. Madame had a drink with Mr Hogbein and Sir Beverly, then said goodnight and went to the lift. Mr Hogbein escorted her, then returned to the lounge, and Madame went up to her room.' He frowned slightly, organising his recollections. 'Then one or two people left to go home, and by about midnight, I'd imagine, there were just Marius, Sir Beverly, myself, Jim Fletcher, Coral Stone...' His eyes traced a visual grouping.

'Mr Hogbein took her into the lift? Or just as far as the lift?'

Craig stopped to think, then looked up at Verdun, a flash of interest in his eyes. 'Yes, just to the lift. I'm pretty sure.'

'Not to her room?'

He hesitated. 'I think he came straight back.'

'From the lift?'

'I—I think so.'

Verdun wrote something, then looked up. 'Anyone else there?'

'Yes, of course. Mave Cardwell was. She's the city's senior drama critic, I suppose you could say.' His tone indicated scant respect. 'And her side-kick, Hal Princeton.'

'Side-kick?'

'Music critic, actually. Heavy drinker, latches on to one rather unpleasantly. But he and Mave are—surprisingly—quite good friends. Like calling to like, perhaps.' He gave the ghost of a smile. 'Though perhaps only in my estimation. I don't think Mave is *really* a drinker. Not to get sozzled, anyway. Hal's a harmless, effeminate twit. Writes quite well. Knows his subject from way back.'

'A musician?'

Craig actually grinned. 'A music critic? If you can reconcile the two.'

Verdun acknowledged the jibe with a faint smile. 'Anyone else?'

'Not that I can recall. Except Clem! Yes, Clem dropped by at some point. Clem Zacaria. Director of the ballet. But he was only there for a few minutes.'

'Tell me about him.'

'Clem?' Craig's eyes were enigmatic. 'He's a ballet dancer with pretensions to creativity! A mad Russian, or so he likes to think. I wouldn't personally let him organise a barn dance, but the ballet company seems to like him.'

'Involved with the festival, of course?'

'In so far as the ballet company has put on a new work, specially created for the occasion.'

'Any good?'

Craig shrugged. 'I'm not into ballet myself. Reports have varied. Modern, *you* know! Heavy metal and reggae with gyrating corpses.'

Verdun gave a minuscule chuckle. 'You are a man of strong affiliations, I suspect. Where do your cultural passions lie?'

Craig raised his eyebrows, staring past the detective. 'I suppose—baroque and classical. 19th century produced some good stuff, but after Beethoven—mostly not for me. I'm not a romantic. 20th—most of it I'd be happy to forget. I like elegance and grace and restraint in my music. I'm not into blatancy.' He caught Verdun's eye. 'I don't suffer from unrestrained passions. I believe in discipline and self-control, even in music.'

Verdun acknowledged the comment with an inclination of the head. 'Well, did you leave the group at all last night?'

'After Madame had gone up? Briefly, if at all. No—I sat and unwound, letting her music live again. People always want to sit and talk after a concert. I like to sit and relive it.'

'It was your period,' Verdun suggested, and Craig nodded.

'Bach! Wonderful! And very sad, of course. But at least there are many superb recordings by which she can be remembered.' He seemed suddenly confused, looking down at his hands. 'That is the immortality that belongs today to all great performers. Their deaths can no longer be the tragedy they were. Once Mozart died, you see—no more Mozart performances. But we can play Ligorno's interpretations for ever, if we wish.' He looked up. 'Perhaps it reduces the tragedy, just a little.'

'On a somewhat lofty level, yes. But she was also a woman, who was brutally attacked.'

'Brutal?' Craig frowned. 'That would be unforgivable.'

'Murder is always brutal,' Verdun commented drily. 'The taking of a life...'

Craig sighed. 'It's a wicked world,' he agreed.

'Do you have any ideas about it?' Verdun asked curiously.

Craig shook his head. 'On the face of it, it's meaningless. A nice woman, a great performer, who would want to hurt her? What was the motive? Robbery? Rape? Revenge? Jealousy? Who inherits her money?' He shrugged. 'I'm not really into detecting.' It was said with dry humour, and Verdun grinned.

'You've touched the main areas! Now it's up to us. Thank you, Mr Schuster. That will do for now.'

Sir Beverly was staring aggressively at the detective sergeant. It was implicit in his manner that he did not expect to be interviewed by anyone less than a full commissioner. Verdun was unmoved.

'Thank you for sparing me the time,' he began, as Sir Beverly ungraciously waved him to an uncomfortably upright chair in his grandiose office—a chair kept exclusively for people he wanted to discompose. Verdun was apparently impervious to such ploys.

'Well, get on with it! Time's money!' the stout knight was saying, and Verdun opened the ubiquitous notebook and clicked his pen, feeling that Sir Beverly might appreciate the classic detective mode.

Briggs, hoping that at some point a moment of drama might erupt to make detecting what he had hoped it would be, shifted slightly on his feet. In his imagination he was savouring the rich taste of a hamburger. He tried not to look at his watch. Surely it was nearly lunchtime? Well, perhaps not—he opened his notebook.

'Just a few questions, Sir Beverly. How long have you known Marius Hogbein?'

'Hogbein? Not expecting him to be tied up in this, are you? Good God, man...!'

'Not at all,' Verdun answered smoothly. 'But I have to discover as much as I can about everyone associated with the case. How long, sir?'

'As long as he's been here. Damn it all, I appointed him! Bloody good value we've had for our money.'

'A good festival director, is he?'

'One of the best. Or he wouldn't have stayed. I'd have seen to that!'

'And Dame Clarissa Payne?'

'Dame Clarissa? What the hell do you want with Clarissa?'

'Nothing, Sir Beverly. Just to know how long you've known her.'

The old man stuttered and swore, and indeed Verdun had not expected to gain anything of value from him. But he had to admit that interviewing the man was an entertainment in itself. At last he broke through the fury.

'You were at the party last night at the hotel after Mme Ligorno left to go to bed. Did you leave the party at any time?'

'Did I…? Did *I* leave…? *Did I leave the party?* Good God, man, are you crazy? Do you know who you're speaking to? Did *I*…!' He seemed to be on the verge of apoplexy, so Verdun closed the notebook and stood up.

'Thank you, sir. You've been very helpful.' He nodded politely and left the room with its fulminating owner, Briggs shadowing him hopefully.

Suddenly, Verdun felt unaccountably depressed. A nice woman murdered, a very special woman, if he was to believe the festival folk; no reason that anyone could see; international repercussions, almost certainly, and the risk of losing the investigation to someone else if he didn't come up with the answers. It was a mug's game! He could have been out in the open air, chasing errant motorists or burning great stacks of cannabis, instead of picking his way through the minefields of people's tender personal prejudices.

'What a mess, eh, Briggs? What do you reckon?'

Briggs lifted a shoulder; he had no idea. Murder among society's drop-outs he could comprehend; murder within the supposedly upper-crust socialites was incomprehensible. 'Drugs?' he suggested. Verdun cast a cool eye on the lad.

'Unlikely.'

'She could have been bringing them in.'

Verdun looked at his watch. 'Lunch, I think.' Suddenly the world seemed brighter to Briggs.

As they sat on a bench outside the concert hall and ate sandwiches from the nearby bar, the detective felt the old sensation rise in him; it was the call of the chase. Somewhere out there, among the hundreds of folks linked, however insubstantially, to the festival, was the one whose gun had been pointed with evil intent, whose steady hand had robbed the world of a woman who had not, it seemed deserved to die.

And he would get that person, or his name was not Nicholas Henry Jarvey Verdun. Which it was!

5

Alicia Hogbein heard her husband's car coming up the driveway. It was most unusual for him to be home at lunchtime, but today was different. When he came through the door from the garage she caught a look on his face of total weariness; but by the time he had walked through into the family room where they normally ate—now that family was no longer at home—he had himself under control.

'Bad morning?' she said, and he nodded.

'Couldn't be anything else. We've all been interviewed by the CIB.'

'Presumably without result?'

'Yes, thank heaven! They don't have any ideas, as far as they're letting on.'

'Do you?'

'Ideas? No.' He shook his head. 'No. Not a thing. How could I? No one involved in the festival could do a thing like that.'

'So you hope.' He stared at her. 'Well, face it, Marius. *Someone* killed her. And it's most likely to be someone who knew her, and whom she knew.'

'Don't even think it!' he groaned. 'I know. You're probably right. There was apparently no sign of a struggle, nothing taken, no

violence shown her except the ultimate violence of murdering her.'
He put his head in his hands. 'Why? For God's sake—why?'

Alicia put some of yesterday's stew on a plate and slid it into the
microwave. 'And—who?' she said deliberately, and set the timer.

As Marius ate the quick lunch, barely tasting it, his mind
ran agitatedly through the days since Camille Ligorno had been
welcomed at the airport. He tried to recall whether anything had
been said, any comment made, about the woman, but he could
recollect nothing but compliments from his staff. Ligorno had
indeed been a pleasure to work with, and to entertain. There were
times when an artiste seemed to put backs up deliberately; he
could remember quite a number, too, who had almost asked to be
murdered for their sheer cussedness! But not this one.

It was a mystery. He was very much afraid it would stay that
way. A motiveless crime! 'They're the worst kind,' he said to Alicia,
who was reading a magazine and only grunted in reply.

When he had finished he shut himself in his study and sat
in his favourite chair, from which he could see the sweep of the
river, now bespeckled with multi-coloured sails scudding before
a brisk breeze. This view normally soothed any tetchy mood,
any momentary depression; but not today. He tried to relax his
shoulders, even took a book down from the shelves and attempted
to read; but all he could see was his vision of what Camille must
have looked like this morning, all the laughter gone from her face,
all the nimbleness from fingers spread wide on the expensive carpet,
all the heart and soul of her spilt like an overturned jug of milk,
irreplaceable—and for what?

All at once he wanted to weep for the arbitrariness of it.
He hoped—how he hoped—that his young people were not
involved. Yet, even as he wished fervently, he dismissed the idea.
It was impossible! He cast his inner eye over them: it was totally
unthinkable that any of them could have been a party to such
wickedness. He would stake his life on it!

Then who? Why? Questions which would perhaps haunt him
for ever. Why couldn't it be someone old and gross like Sir Beverly?
Some 'dero' slinking in through the back door and climbing the

stairs in search of booze? Some unmitigated clot like Clem Zacaria? Perhaps a rejected lover who had followed her across the world until the opportunity for revenge offered itself, somewhere, anywhere! 'But not at *my* festival!' Marius mourned inwardly as he backed the car out on to the driveway. 'Find somewhere else for your maniac activities!'

Mave Cardwell and Hal Princeton were sitting together in the bar of one of the better hotels—but not the one where the police investigation was. They not infrequently lunched together, combining their love for gossip with a strange kind of mutual detestation. Mave disliked Hal's drinking habits, but tolerated them for the morsels of information he could produce; Hal, sensing her dislike, oddly enjoyed the sense of impending friction that Mave's proximity gave him.

'So what's the answer?' Mave was saying, eyeing a toasted sandwich with some suspicion before biting into it. 'God knows what they put in these things, darling!'

Hal emptied his glass before speaking. Finally he said, 'Means, motive, opportunity. Isn't that the classic formula? Well, we all had the opportunity, I suppose. It wouldn't have been too difficult to slip upstairs and do her in. How long would it take, first to last? Five minutes? Six, maybe, if you used the stairs. 'Knock-knock, bang-bang!' He took a fork to the baked potato on his plate, pushing the salad to one side. 'Means? Who has a gun?'

'I do,' Mave said. 'It belonged to my husband.'

'Which one?'

'Husband or gun?' she asked with a wicked leer. 'Last husband! The one who lost his head over a bit of fluff. He took my money but left the pistol. Probably hoped I'd use it. But I'm saving it.'

'For him?'

'You never know. He might come back one day. When the fluff gets old and tatty. And then I might use the gun.'

Hal regarded her with interest. 'You wouldn't, would you? After all this time?'

Mave sighed gustily. 'No, why bother? He's only a man, after all. Who needs him?'

Hal giggled slightly. 'Oh, I wouldn't say that, dear. Somebody loves him.' He watched her thoughtfully as a piece of tomato slid out of the sandwich and fell on to her lap. 'Is the gun a working model?'

'How would I know?' Mave swore at the tomato and wiped her skirt angrily. 'I doubt if I could find it now. Even if I wanted to.'

'So *you* didn't kill Ligorno?'

She stared at him with disgust. 'Do me a favour, Hal! Murder a real artiste? When there's thousands that no one would miss?'

'That leaves motive. Who would gain from killing her?'

'No one! That's the short answer. Certainly no one here. It can't do anything but harm—except the publicity.' She grinned at him. 'Did you see Marius's face when I said that? He was ropable!'

'Then it's a totally pointless crime, and therefore the police are most likely unable to clear it up. They like some logic in their malefactors. It will turn out to be someone who went up to her room, shot her, and then left. And if there's nothing to link him to her, what hope have the flat-footed ones got?'

They stared gloomily into their empty glasses. It seemed a pity, when something really stirring happened, that it should simply die away from inanition.

'Same again!' Hal called to the barman.

6

Coral stacked up the work she had tried desperately hard to finish, when no one around her seemed to have anything to do but moon around, waiting for an imminent arrest. It was near enough to the end of the day, and she had to wash her hair and get herself into something suitable for watching a performance of erotic puppets. Though it was difficult to say what might indeed be correct wear for such an esoteric display.

As she pulled the cover over her computer the door swung open and Clem Zacaria swept into the room. Coral had sometimes wondered what he was like when he was on his own. Did his bubble pop, the balloon deflate, so that he became an ordinary mortal? No one knew. The people she had asked had only seen him in company, and company could be as little as one to get Clem going.

Perhaps there *was* no one inside him, she pondered, wishing he would go away; perhaps he was only an empty shell, a clockwork husk, wound up in the morning and only collapsing, spent, when he arrived home at night.

'Can I help you, Clem?'

'Where is police?'

'They've gone. They've been here all day, but now they've gone.'

'Ha! So! They 'ave finish?'

'Oh, I doubt it. I don't think they have a clue who did it.'

'So they are back tomorrow in morning?'

'I expect so. Why?'

'I am not liking police. They are searching alway into dark secrets.'

'What dark secrets?' Coral grinned at him. 'Who has dark secrets?' It was impossible to take him seriously.

Clem stared around him as if he expected to find a spy hidden in a filing cabinet. 'All peoples are 'aving dark secrets. I myself 'ave dark secrets. I do not wish the police to know zem. I shall not tell!' He took up a heroic pose.

Coral groaned. 'Oh, Clem, stop acting. Be serious!'

'I *am* serious.' He gave her a baleful look. 'I am *alway* serious. Zacaria do not joke. I 'ave Russian blood.'

'All the Russians I've met have had a sense of humour.' Coral searched in her bag for lipstick and perfume. Zacaria flashed his eyes at her.

'Zis is for proletariat, for peasants. Sense of humour to deaden pain and suffering. I am aristocrat, and I am alway serious.'

'Clem, pirouette off and let me get home. I've been working hard all day.'

'I too must work. But my vibrations, zey are *distraits*. It is necessary to 'ave calm, repose for the soul.'

'There's some vodka in the drinks cupboard,' she said, without looking up. Clem Zacaria gave her a brief but winning smile, which she missed.

'You are good girl, Coral. You understand the needs of the artistic spirit.' He walked to the door with the peculiarly stilted movements of the ballet dancer and paused for effect, but she ignored him.

'Leave some for Marius,' she called as he closed the door behind him. When he had gone she stopped and lifted her head to stare out of the window at the distant river. 'Who?' she thought. 'And how? And why? *Why?* Clem? Surely not. Jim? Craig? Who else? Hal Princeton? Would a music critic ever be able to destroy a wonderful talent like Ligorno's? Never!'

She drove her mind on mercilessly. 'Marius?' She couldn't see it. Apart from the damage it would do to the festival, Marius wasn't the type. Was he? What was the type? Who in his right mind could possibly…or *her* right mind, she told herself. An unbalanced woman could have done it.

But all the time the question was there: why? With Camille Ligorno barely known to any of them, how could it have happened? Nothing taken from the room, no apparent motive… she put her head into her hands. The police *must* come up with something—quickly!

'The flowers!' Mave said suddenly. 'Of course—the flowers!'

'What about them?' Hal was sitting on a riverside bench while Mave stomped up and down the pathway, deep in creative thought.

'They must have come from somewhere. Find out who bought the flowers, and…!' She snapped her fingers triumphantly. Hal's face took on an unusually solemn look.

'Are you sure you want to know, Mave, ol' dear?'

She turned to look straight at him. 'Was it you?'

He shook his head without offence. 'No, it wasn't. But it was someone. Do you really want to know who?'

She thought about it for a while, then nodded vigorously. 'Yes, I do! We *have* to know, don't we? Speaking as a drama critic—who wants a play without a denouement? We can't be left hanging for ever.' Hal winced. She gathered her handbag to her, searching for sunglasses. 'I'm going to speak to that bloke Vernon, Vaughan, whatsisname…?'

'Verdun.'

'I'm going to ask him about the flowers.'

'Don't get your fingers burnt, dear,' Hal said as she left in a waft of pungent perfume, a flowing scarf barely keeping up with her. He watched her go, then made his way to the nearest bar. What did it matter, anyway? Ligorno was gone, and nothing would bring her back. His review of her wondrous final concert would be savagely cut by the sub-editors to make room for the news of her sordid death. He wondered why he bothered.

That odd woman, the drama critic, burst through the door like a whirlwind, and Verdun regarded her with a cool and detached eye which had no effect on her. He noticed among the draperies the scrawny arms and blotched hands of incipient old age, bedecked with bangles and rings in primitive art style, chunks of silver adorned with gems as big as pebbles. All a bit much, he thought, but these arty types are all the same! 'Mr Vaughan!' she clarioned across the room.

'Verdun. Nick Verdun.' He stood courteously.

'Nick, then. Look—just a little thought that came to me over the flesh-pots. The flowers!'

'Yes?'

'Well—where did they come from? Who bought them? Surely it would help if you knew?'

He smiled, quite graciously. 'Do sit down. Yes, the flowers! Bought by the hotel for their fifth floor floral arrangements. One at each end of the long corridor, under the windows. A different colour scheme for each floor. On Mme Ligorno's floor it was deep reds and pinks. So—roses and carnations. The murderer must have taken them from the vase, concealed the gun behind them, knocked at the door and killed her as she stood there. They weren't missed until this morning because the lights are turned low at night. But one of the maids had told the manager before the body had been found. It seems that people do sometimes meddle with the flower arrangements, especially if they've been celebrating.' He smiled again and she leaned back, nodding approvingly.

'You don't miss much.'

'It's my job.'

'Well, then…' She thought for a moment. 'Whose gun was used to fire the fatal shot? Do you know that?'

'Not yet. The results haven't come in. But there was no trace of it in the room, nor anywhere in the hotel. It was probably quite a powerful weapon, so almost certainly had a silencer. The noise it would have made otherwise would have been enormous in an enclosed corridor, People would have been tumbling out of their beds.'

She nodded slowly, eyeing him pensively. 'It's going to be a tricky one, isn't it?'

'Certainly looks like it, Miss Cardwell.'

'Mave!' she said, leaning across to pat his hand. 'We're all in this together, Nick. Let's not stand on ceremony.'

He watched her go. She was odd, almost comical, but she was shrewd. Perhaps, if she was also observant, she might prove to be quite useful. It made a change from your average criminal 'grass', anyway.

And, perhaps, there was more behind her questions than was evident. He reminded himself not to be carried away by her age or oddities. This was a murder investigation and until further notice Mave was a suspect.

'Pity!' he said aloud.

By the end of that first day everyone was a trifle on edge. Mave Cardwell was due at the all-black 'Pygmalion', Marius and Alicia and Hal Princeton were booked to attend a recital of ancient Japanese music at the university, and Dame Clarissa and Sir Beverly were guests of honour at a display of early gold-rush photographs.

'This feller going to solve the damn murder, then eh?' Sir Beverly barked as his path crossed the dame's; and she, well up to form, answered him in ringing tones that brought instant silence to the gallery.

'We must hope so, Beverly. Otherwise we're *all* under suspicion.' The prospect almost seemed to please her.

'*We're* all right!' he snorted, harrumphing madly. 'We were at the party. Anyone could vouch.'

'But not after midnight, Beverly.' She poked his ample short-front. 'Not after twelve! Where were you then, eh? Did anyone see you?'

'Now, look here, Clarissa...' he began; but his hosts, seeing disaster threatening, separated the two old antagonists and kept them apart for the rest of the evening.

'But where, indeed, was he?' Dame Clarissa wondered, as she studied a family group of dirt-bespattered, surly miners appropriately caught for posterity in muddy sepia. 'How courageous these people were!' she exclaimed to her hosts. 'How poverty-stricken!' She moved to a more ornate photograph of an upright, elderly woman with a steely eye that transfixed her so that she came to a sudden halt.

'Where were *you?*' the eye seemed to be saying. 'Can you prove where *you* were? Judge not,' the woman commanded her sternly over the years, 'that ye be not judged!'

'You're quite right,' Dame Clarissa muttered. 'Leave it to the police.' Her escort leaned towards her to catch her words of wisdom. 'What a very striking lady! Do we know who she was?'

Marius had dreaded the recital's interval, with some justice, for he was immediately surrounded by a throng of well-wishers and scandal-mongers, and eventually took refuge in the manager's office.

'They're like vultures,' he said to Alicia. 'Hyenas after the kill! Ghouls!'

Alicia sighed. 'They're just excited. Don't make a fuss. Looked at from their angle, it's the most exciting thing that's happened all festival.'

'Oh, *thank you* very much!' He glared at her. 'That's *very* nice. A cultural festival, this is, not a blood-letting. Perhaps we should hold a gladiatorial contest next year. Dip a few Christians in tar and burn them as torches!'

'Well, you'd certainly get the crowds,' she said calmly.

'Et tu, Brut*ess*?' he growled, sullen.

'Why—who else?' She was looking through a pictorial calendar of the Yorkshire Dales, yawning slightly with ennui.

'Sir Bloody Beverly! *He* thinks that all that matters is bums on seats. You'd better arrange it with him.'

'You can't change human nature, my dear Marius. It's only a matter of years since people in London used to take their children to watch public hangings—for the fun of it. I doubt if we're any different.' She yawned again.

'Are you *bored*?' he snarled, thoroughly out of temper. She nodded. 'Well, I'm really sorry. I split a gut all year to find new and interesting performers, and *my wife is bored*! Good grief!' he said, self-pityingly. 'Why do I bother?'

'Don't make such a fuss.' Alicia took out her powder compact and dabbed at her nose. 'You know I hate Japanese music. You should be grateful to me for coming.'

He held on to himself with an effort. He had no right to be obnoxious; it was true, she supported him to the hilt, always had done. But without being carried away by it—that was what got him. She spent the whole of the festival going where he went, making the right noises, smiling at people, the perfect director's wife—and even now, after years and years of it, he didn't actually know how she felt about it. 'Alicia...' he began

She turned and smiled at him, quite warmly. 'Time to go back. The bell's ringing.' He followed her to the door, and put out a hand to her.

'Alicia—you aren't bored all the time, are you?'

She smiled again, quickly, opening the door. 'Not all the time—no,' she said gently, and was absorbed into the crowd.

7

Some slept peacefully that night, some tossed and turned. It was very humid, with heavier weather expected for the following day. One lay staring at the ceiling, thinking, calculating, planning; sleep, when it came, arrived smoothly, and there were no recognisable dreams.

Marius got up several times—glasses of water, visits to the bathroom, anything to break the movie film inside his head. Alicia heard him but did not interfere. He would work it out in his own way.

Coral Stone checked and double-checked the locks on doors and windows of her bijou town house. She had suddenly conceived the notion that perhaps Ligorno's death was the systematic massacre of festival adherents; even though she discounted the idea as hysterical nonsense she found herself listening to every creak and groan as the house settled for the night, transmuting them into forced entries as a prelude to assassination. Eventually she pulled the dressing table across the bedroom door and fell asleep at last with the light on. She dreamt she was being propositioned by a ten-foot puppet.

Hal and Mave slept (in their own beds in separate suburbs) the sleep of the well-lubricated. Hal's review of the Japanese recital had been delivered before the deadline, and was carefully non-committal; the performers' abundant skills had balanced against the alien quality of their music to incline his judgement slightly in their favour; but he had to wash away the taste in the nearest bar for half an hour afterwards. His repose was deep and dreamless.

Mave, exhausted from coping with the complexities of black-American accents in a 'Pygmalion' transported to the deep south, wrote her copy and went home thankfully. She removed her make-up and sat staring at herself in her bedroom mirror. What she saw was depressing enough to make her want to cry: an elderly face with coarsened skin and wrinkles turning to folds; eye-whites gone liverish, and a startlingly black mop of hair above.

'I should have gone grey,' she told herself. 'Gracefully!' She turned away and hid herself under her purple striped quilt, her head throbbing with old age and too much gin. When sleep came it presented a distorted picture of Hal Princeton advancing on her with a gun that turned into a huge ball-point pen. 'Write!' he was saying. 'Write! Write! Write till you drop....'

'Go away, you silly old bugger!' she said crossly, and dreamed that he became Cary Grant and she a slender Indian princess. She wriggled down into the bed and let him have his way with her.

Dawn was beautiful for those who were up to see it. Marius, sleepy at last, resisted the temptation to close the curtains and relapse into slumber; he let himself out of the house and wandered down the river where the undisturbed water was silken, to watch the early birds, feathered and human, in their search for rewards.

The only 'worm' he wanted at this moment was to know that yesterday had been a bad dream; but when he strode briskly home again, revived by the cool air and a sense of self-discipline, the rolled-up newspaper on his front lawn assured him that the dream was the reality. '*World famous pianist slain*' said the headline; there were photographs of Camille Ligorno, smiling graciously at the camera in the way that he remembered—the way she would never smile again.

A picture of Marius himself on page two had been taken some years before ('they might keep their files up to date', he thought grumpily). '*Festival director Marius Hogbein devastated by shocking loss to world of international music,*' said the caption. He could not recall having used the words 'devastated' or 'shocking', but let it pass. There had been reporters everywhere. How could one remember what one had said in the stress of the moment?

They ate on the tiny terrace, he and Alicia, companionably silent, reading their newspaper (half each); and it was eye of the cyclone, the false calm before a very real storm.

'What today?' Alicia asked.

'I have to meet Alessandri at the airport at midday.'

'He won't cancel?'

'Cancel?' said Marius, to whom the idea came as a shock. 'Why should he cancel?'

Alicia shrugged. 'Might think this is a dangerous place for pianists.'

Marius snorted. 'Don't be daft! One murder isn't a massacre.'

'All massacres start with one murder!' She collected the dishes and carried them indoors. Marius shouted after her.

'That's a stupid thing to say. Really stupid, that is! Starts my day off with a bang, that does.' He opened the paper angrily, to see a headline above a group of blurred, smiling faces: '*US gunman wipes out church choir*'.

'Oh, *lor!*' he said bitterly. 'What's the world coming to?'

Coral, her night-time ordeal safely over, rang him. 'People are ringing up,' she said, her voice trembling slightly. 'From all over the place.'

'Where?'

'Well—Sydney! And San Francisco, Ottawa, Rome—that's so far, and I don't see it stopping. Newspapers, mainly. And someone called Don Basilio from Paris.'

'Don Basilio? Are you sure?'

'It *sounded* like Don Basilio,' she said uncertainly. 'But it wasn't a good line.'

'What did he want?'

'I couldn't tell. He was speaking in Italian. Or something. I think.'

Marius sighed. He put the receiver down and stood for a moment, wondering where to start. When Alicia came into the

room he turned towards her and held out his hands, and she came
to him and took them. 'Bear with me,' he said humbly. 'It's been a
big shock.'

She slid her arms around him and held him against her. 'Don't
I always?' she said, rubbing her cheek against his hair.

'Am I so awful?' he said, pulling away to look at her.

She nodded cheerfully, without passion. 'Yes! Until the festival's
over. So what else is new?'

He gave a short, humourless laugh. 'A corpse is what's new,'
he said, packing his briefcase. He kissed her quickly. 'I don't know
when I'll be home.'

She watched him go. Perhaps he would never know, even
suspect, how much of his success was generated from her batteries.
If she were to run out of power, where would he be? She sighed as
the car disappeared round the bend. What would it have been like
to be married to a banker, with regular hours? Or a butcher? Or a
school-teacher? She shuddered. Well, perhaps not a school-teacher!

The phone rang. 'Clarissa Payne here!' it boomed at her, and
she pulled a face. 'Just wanted to say what a shocking thing, my
dear. Hope you're not letting it get you down? Good! That man of
yours will need all the help he can get while this wretched affair
works itself out. But he's strong—and he's got you. And if it means
anything—he's got me! I envy you, my dear. Marius is a quite
wonderful man—highly gifted, good to look at—and well matched
by you, my dear. Well matched! Well, it's been nice to have a little
chat. Chin up, and don't weaken. Bye-bye!'

Alicia held the receiver for a moment, quite still. It had not
been necessary to say a word. 'She's in love with Marius!' she
thought, not sure whether to giggle or weep. But when she was
making the bed later she found she was singing. '...*high as a flag...*'
she carolled, punching the pillows. '*I'm in love with a wo-o-onderful
gu-uy!*'

'For you,' Coral said, pointing to the phone.

'Who?' Marius asked, and she shrugged.

'That Don Basilio again. Paris.'

Marius lifted the receiver. It was a very bad line. 'Hullo! Hullo! Are you there?'

'Yes,' said a faint voice. 'I have a call for you from...' The phone crackled suddenly.

'Is that Don Basilio?' Marius asked, resisting the temptation to shout.

'Yes—who is that? I have a call for you, Australia...'

Crackle-crackle! 'I can't hear you.' Marius enunciated with penetrating care. 'Who is that?'

It *sounded* like 'Don Basilio'. But after more twitterings the line suddenly cleared, and a deep female voice said, 'Rhonda Sillitoe here, in Paris. I'm Paris correspondent for the London Trumpeter, and I've just heard that the divine Ligorno has got herself slaughtered.'

Marius winced. 'Someone has murdered her,' he agreed unwillingly.

'Who am I speaking with?' asked the lady. 'I want Mary Hogbein. I believe you have some sort of little festival going on...'

'*I am Marius Hogbein!*' he exploded. 'I am director of a long-standing and prestigious festival, and for your information Mme Ligorno is not the only international artiste to appear for us...'

'Isn't Mary Hogbein there? Well, can *you* give me some info? Something quotable about Ligorno, or the weather or something. Anything! I'll see Mary gets a mention. I just want one par for my article on the lady. She was here last week, you know. Can you get hold of Ms Hogbein for me?'

'No!' roared Marius. 'She was murdered too! Stabbed—in the back!' He slammed the phone down. Coral came and stood cautiously just inside the door. She shook her head, questioning.

'Not—Don Basilio?'

'Rhonda Sillitoe, you idiot! Some crass female journo who writes for some ought-to-be-pulped ghastly rag in London!' He swung his chair round so that he was staring into the corner of the room. Behind him came a strange noise, something between a sniff and a hiccup, a kind of lonely, distraught noise. 'Are you crying?' he said, not daring to turn round.

'Not exactly,' said Carol in a choked voice, and ran.

Jim Fletcher and Craig Schuster alighted from adjacent buses; Jim waited for Craig to catch up with him.

'Beastly hot and muggy,' he said. Craig nodded. He was never chatty. 'Wonder what faces us today.' They walked in silence for half a minute. 'What do *you* think?' Jim said at last, glancing sideways at his companion.

'About what?'

'About the—this Ligorno thing. *You* know! Do you have any theory why anyone should want to kill her?'

'It's always been my belief that a motiveless crime would be the hardest to solve. What would you hang the evidence on? Perhaps we're going to see that theory proved.'

'I hope not. We don't want an unsolved murder hanging around our necks.' He shivered. 'You'd never know who...'

'Or why.'

'It might have been anyone. You, me, Marius...'

'Coral?'

Jim was shocked. 'Oh, surely not Coral?'

'I don't see why not. If we're likely contenders, why not she?'

'I don't think that's very nice. Besides, why would she?'

'Why would I? Why would you? Or Marius? Just because we're men? You don't have much opinion of your own sex.'

Jim fell silent, his mind sliding off in other directions. 'This is going to make one hell of a stink with all the other places she was booked to play this season. For that reason alone...'

They arrived at the outer door of the festival offices, and within they could see the solid form of Nick Verdun. 'Ah,' Craig said, 'the gendarmes are here already. What more can we tell them?' He glanced at Jim, mockery in his eyes; but Jim was white-faced. 'Don't let them *worry* you. They have their job to do. Once they've finished with us we can get back to whatever has to be done next.' He acknowledged Verdun with a nod. 'In your case, getting Marius down to preparing a proper press release.'

8

One of the worst things, Coral was finding, was the barely perceptible cloud of suspicion now hanging over the festival office. Barely perceptible because they were all good friends, and one doesn't easily categorise one's friends as potential murderers.

But now and then, when the inevitable breaks in activity occurred—those moments when, under normal circumstances, someone would be sure to say 'Anyone want coffee?'—memories would flood in, and there would be an uneasiness, no one really wanting to discuss the case, no one able to ignore it.

Somehow it was easier when Nick Verdun was around. Then, an air of officialdom cloaked the whole rotten business; strangely, Verdun assumed a kind of responsibility for what had happened— and what, if his endeavours were successful, must still happen; an authoritative finger pointing, an arrest, and then the long-drawn traumas of trial, conviction, sentence. It was enough to make one shudder.

Craig walked through her office. 'Marius in?' he asked, and she nodded. On an impulse she took a deep breath and said, 'What do you think, Craig? What's going to happen?'

He stared down at her for a moment, and she deduced from a faint withdrawal in his eyes that he, too, was affected; the nonchalant, balanced pose was as fragile as her own. 'No one knows, do they, Carol? It looks like the perfect mystery—so far.'

As he closed Marius's door behind him a gale of sound and fury in the entrance materialised as Clem Zacaria at his most trying.

'I do not speak no more to the police,' he was declaiming. 'No, no, NO! I 'ave ze performance tonight, and ze soul must be at rest. At rest, mon ami!' He erupted into Coral's room, the dark-suited figure of Verdun close behind him. 'Expliquez, chère Carol, to zis enemy of ze people zat my soul must be left in peace today…!'

'Clem!' she cried, trying to penetrate his tragic aura. 'Clem! We all have to help the police. How else can we find Mme Ligorno's murderer?' She shrugged helplessly at Verdun.

'I have no wish to disturb the peace of your soul, sir,' he was saying with patient reason. 'Just to ask you a few simple questions. Ten minutes of your time, no more.'

'I cannot fill my mind with such—such *sordid* matters.' His gestures threatened a bowl of flowers on the desk, and Coral moved them out of reach. 'I am above such things.'

'Then you are very fortunate, sir,' Verdun said. 'Most of us can't afford to be so high-minded.' He paused for a moment. 'Perhaps I should mention that it would have been within my powers to have closed the festival down. Then there would have been no performances tonight. My superiors allowed it to continue running because they saw how important it was.'

Zacaria regarded him swiftly, and the detective noted that the surreal personality lifted fractionally to reveal an unexpectedly shrewd pair of eyes. Then the moment was gone.

'*He* can tell a hawk from a handsaw!' thought Verdun, whose education had not been entirely wasted. 'He'll bear watching.'

'Ten minutes!' Zacaria said, suddenly and imperiously. 'No more.' He led the way into an empty room, Verdun following with his notebook at the ready. Coral watched them go. Jim, entering the room at that moment, joined her. As the door closed he sat down suddenly as if his legs had given way.

'When you see it on TV,' (his voice shook infinitesimally),'you don't get the whole picture, do you? It always looks so clean-cut, so predictable. The goodies are goodies, and the baddies are baddies. And even if a goody is a baddy, there's always something that gives him away. A dreadful tie or something. No one can feel sorry for a criminal who wears dreadful ties!' He laughed, his face taut. Coral tried to smile encouragingly, but the smile stuck to her teeth and emerged as a nervous grimace.

'You know what's really awful? It's Camille Ligorno herself. That lovely person. She's lying in some—some *cool-room* in the city, all those skills gone, all that charm and elegance finished, already nearly forgotten because we're all more concerned with *whodunit.*' She bit her lip. 'Worse! *Which of us dunit?* It has to be someone associated with the festival. Doesn't it?'

She looked at him imploringly, willing him to give her a solution that would return them to the status quo, when they were all hard-working entrepreneurs and Ligorno was a living, breathing artiste—not a carcass in a refrigerated morgue. But Jim could not meet her eyes. 'Doesn't it, Jim?'

'It may look like it,' he said at length. 'How do we know? Perhaps it was international terrorists.'

'But they always claim their own violence, don't they? Otherwise there's no point.'

'Drugs?' He shrugged. '*I* don't know. Perhaps?'

'Smuggling? Dealing? Ligorno?' Carol laughed sharply, unamused. 'Ligorno? Oh, come on, Jim!'

He stood up, offended. 'Don't you think the police will look at all those things? After all, they're just as likely as that one of us is a—a murderer.'

Coral squeezed her brow with her fingers. She had a headache coming on. After a struggle with herself she said, 'You're right, of course, Jim. I'm sorry. We didn't really know her. Who can tell what sort of a person she was in fact? Travelling around the world like that, maybe she could have had links with—well, with anyone.'

'She was Italian,' Jim said, accepting the olive branch. 'Perhaps—Mafia?'

Coral's eyes followed him. Her bright image of Camille Ligorno was being tarnished, and she could do nothing about it. And the worst, she knew, was yet to come.

'That night,' Verdun was saying patiently. 'I just need to know where everyone was during the period which covered Mme Ligorno's murder. We are establishing alibis, sir—or the lack of them.'

'"ow can I say?' Zacaria was still outraged. '"ow can you think I 'ave mind small enough to make timetable? My mind is full of thoughts ze most *formidables*, ze most *enormes*. 'ow shall I descend to ze level of a *policeman?*' He expressed the final word with exquisite disgust.

'It must be very difficult for you, sir,' agreed Verdun equably. 'But *chacun a son gout,* as they say. After the Lord Mayor's show, the dustcart. A favourite expression of my mother's.' He smiled apologetically.

'I am not understanding you.'

'Someone has to clean up the messes.' Verdun shrugged half-humorously. 'A world full of ballet dancers wouldn't be very practicable.'

'Ha!' Zacaria glared at him. ('Gaining time,' Verdun noted out of long experience.) 'Zere would be much *jalousie*, much stab in back. Artistes are *très* temperamental.'

'And shootings in the head?' Verdun said, suddenly deadly serious. Zacaria, caught in a moment of self-glorification, stopped his posturing and narrowed his eyes, regarding his opponent with a long and analytical stare. Verdun met his gaze unflinchingly.

'You think you trap me, ha? You trap Zacaria? Zat is not possible. Zacaria is free spirit. He snaps his fingers at traps!' He did so.

'But he gets the message, doesn't he?' Verdun countered, entering into the third-person game with ease. 'He knows that I have my job to do. That no one can with impunity destroy an artiste and expect to get away with it. He knows,' he went on, warming to the new ploy, 'that it is necessary for the police all over the world to protect the artistic community from violence, to see that they have—how did you put it, sir?—rest for their souls.' He smiled winningly. 'Now, Mr Zacaria, where were you between eleven and twelve-thirty on the night of Mme Ligorno's death?'

'But zis I 'ave already told!' Zacaria exclaimed plaintively. 'Why you persecute me again?'

'Come, sir! Persecution? Nothing, surely, is too much effort to bring to justice the person who destroyed that fine artistic soul?' He waited hopefully.

'Ze soul,' Zacaria said with infinite wisdom, 'cannot be destroyed.' He leaned back in his chair and crossed his arms—defiant, it seemed to Verdun. That patient researcher into the human psyche took a deep, slow breath, directed a penetrating eye on his adversary, and poised his pen over his notebook.

'You visited the post-concert party in the hotel lounge,' he began in flat, official tones. 'That would have been at...?' He looked down his nose: and Zacaria, seeing steel in the other's gaze, gave in gracefully.

9

'There's a few papers to sign,' Craig said, placing them on the desk in front of Marius. 'Some letters, ditto. The contract for next year's chamber orchestra. That's about it for now. And, of course,' he glanced at his watch, 'it's nearly time to meet Alessandri.'

'Already?' Marius checked the time with his desk clock. 'Where did the morning go? Where's Zacaria? He was supposed to want to see me.'

'I think I heard him come in.' He put his head out of the door. 'Seen Clem, Coral?'

'In with Mr Verdun.' She nodded towards the closed room.

'In with Verdun,' Craig repeated. Marius laughed drily.

'Half his luck! No one's ever conducted a reasonable conversation with Clem yet!' He scribbled his signature, running his eye swiftly over the documents. 'Life must go on, I suppose.'

The chore completed, he leaned back and regarded Craig thoughtfully. 'Funny how you always think you've reached the limits of your capacity, and then life piles on something more and you find you expand to fit it.' He saw incomprehension on the other's face. 'I thought worrying about the festival was an over-full-time job. Now I find I can worry about this wretched business. Do you suppose they've got any ideas yet? Silly question—how would you know?'

Craig shook his head. 'But I know what you mean. I thought my hands were full before my—before my wife died. Afterwards—well, I found that one has limitless capacities, for all sorts of things.' His face closed in. 'And time to think.'

They were silent, frozen in their emotions. At length Marius stirred. 'It must have been a very terrible time for you. If you ever want to talk about it…?'

Craig shook his head. 'It's over. I believe one has to go forward. Decide on the goal, and then…' He made a sharply-thrusting gesture with his right hand as rigid as a cleaver. 'Then you go for it!' He caught Marius's eye and flashed a quick, bitter smile. 'I learnt that when I was doing science. It felt wrong—I knew I should be next door, in the music school. But I spent two years battering my head against a wall of science, and it took a revelation, a reversal of thinking, to put me where I should have been all along.'

He gathered the signed documents together and put them in their folder. 'I vowed I would never do it again—no more woolly thinking! I promised myself not to waste my life—it's the one great sin, wasting one's life.' He raised an eyebrow in query, and after a moment Marius nodded, morose.

'I agree. And the worst kind of waste of life must be murder, the waste of someone else's life.'

'But she—Ligorno—didn't waste her *own* life!' Craig said eagerly. 'She lived fully. She's immortal, if you like. No one can take that away from her. She was at her peak. At least *she* will never be one of those sad figures we see, travelling round the world interminably, losing the golden sparkle, on a circuit for eternity. Unable to give up the international treadmill because they can't afford to—or can't face retirement without the roar of the crowd.' He stopped suddenly. 'Sorry, Marius. I got carried away.' He moved towards the door.

'Interesting point of view,' Marius said, frowning. 'Not quite a reason for murder, but interesting.'

Craig gave him an enigmatic look. 'Alessandri,' he said, tapping his watch. 'Don't leave it too late.'

The plane was not on time, of course, they never are when it matters. Marius paced the huge foyer on the international airport, waiting with butterflies in his stomach, hating the inactivity.

This was another first visit. Piers Alessandri, tall, handsome, darling of music-lovers the world over through his constant TV appearances and a succession of golden discs, had never before been enticed to Australia (a country which he privately believed was inhabited by kangaroos and sheep farmers). His imminent arrival was a tremendous feather in Marius's cap, and a noteworthy coup for the festival.

None of this brought Marius any comfort as he pounded the foyer floor. He had met the great man once, in Vienna two years before, when they had finalised the contract that was now about to be honoured. But since then, of course, Marius had been careless enough to lose another star of the pianoforte, and he was dreading what Alessandri might say.

The doors slid open to reveal the tanned elegance of a man well over sixty, his silvery hair glinting impeccably above the waiting crowd. It had not occurred to Marius, in his confused state of mind, that many of those waiting were Alessandri fans, and he was taken aback by the rustle of anticipation and then a mutter that rose to a cry of welcome. Alessandri stopped and faced his audience, his smile urbane, his hands raised in acknowledgement.

A young woman broke ranks and shoved her autograph book under his nose; and for a moment a few entranced members of the milling crowd stood close enough to him to smell the expensive aftershave, even in some cases to touch the casually elegant sweater he wore slung around his neck. He could have been a retired tennis ace, a Hollywood legend; but he was Alessandri, and Marius was responsible for him!

He pushed forward, chin thrust out belligerently. 'Excuse me! Excuse me...' He elbowed his way through, caring not whose feet he trampled, and found himself, breathless and irritable, at the front of the queue.

'Do you *mind*!' a young woman said, giving him a push. 'We was here first. Wait your turn!'

'Signor Alessandri!' he exclaimed, feeling hot and untidy by comparison with the flawlessness facing him. The Italian threw his arms wide with a well-turned expression of pleasure.

'Mr Hogbein! My good friend! Here we are, you see, sound and safe at last. It is good to see you.' They shook hands formally, and Marius put a hand on the baggage trolley, which was moving slowly towards them, invisibly propelled, its wiry frame piled high with very exclusive travel goods.

'Let me take this. I have a car waiting.'

From behind the trolley emerged a young woman, a dusky beauty with legs to her waist, wearing a plain burnt-orange shift that screamed haute couture, and lavishly decorated with lumps of gold, which (had they not been true metal) would have demonstrated an appalling lack of taste. Marius had no doubt they were genuine.

She smiled at him, lazily sliding her eyes up and down his body before allowing herself to be enveloped in Alessandri's proprietorial embrace.

'My secretary, Tabitha,' he said, gazing down at her with a sort of detached lust. '*Tabitha* means 'gazelle'. Appropriate, don't you think? Say hullo to Mr Hogbein, carissima.'

She held out a scarlet-taloned claw, and Marius took it nervously. 'Hi-i…!' she said in a long-drawn manner, accompanied by a lowering of lashes that brought to mind Marilyn Monroe at her best. Or worst! It depended how it took you.

He was totally confused. As the loving couple drifted out into the humid afternoon, unencumbered by luggage (which Marius was steering after them on a trolley with a mind of its own), he tried to remember if there had ever, at any time, been the slightest suggestion that Alessandri would be accompanied, either by a secretary—or by what seemed a great deal more likely. And he was sure that there had not.

In the car, as they sped into the city, he tried to put his problem to them.

'I had not expected Miss—er…Miss…'

'Tabitha,' she said, sliding a little closer to her companion.

'Tabitha!' he said, unwillingly. Giving a name to her only seemed to confirm the embarrassing fact that she was there, her long legs provocatively stretched out to his fascinated gaze, her jewellery like open day at Fort Knox. 'You see,' he said, turning deliberately towards Alessandri, 'we have made no preparation for your—companion.'

'My secretary,' Alessandri corrected him.

'Don't worry about little me,' she murmured. 'I take up so little room. I'll just curl up in a corner. You'll hardly even know I'm there.'

Suddenly spiteful, Marius said, 'Will you require a typewriter?' Tabitha laughed, something between a purr and a growl.

'I don't type, darling. I'm not employed to type.' She turned huge eyes up to Alessandri's doting face. 'I'm more of a—personal—private secretary! Isn't that right, Piers?'

Piers Alessandri, world-famous pianist, honorary doctor of five universities, winner of golden disc awards for more than twenty years, respected authority and long-time womaniser, dropped a besotted kiss on the end of her snub brown nose.

'It is very right, kitten! Very private—and very personal.'

Marius stifled a deep and anguished sigh. There were still ten kilometres to go.

'And now tell me,' said Alessandri suddenly, 'what have you done to Ligorno?'

'Don't ask!' Marius said in answer to Coral's questions. He groaned. 'To think I've looked forward to this for two years!' He rubbed his face nervously. 'I may not survive this festival. Coffee, Coral, please.'

'But what happened?' she said as he emptied his cup. She sat on the other side of the desk, watching him with anxious sympathy. He told her.

'Is she awful?' she asked when he had finished.

'Gross! Oh, *lor* —haven't we enough problems?'

'What will you do?'

'I've already done some of it.' He gave a hollow laugh. 'I told them at the hotel that all her expenses are to be billed to him.' He groaned again. 'How are the mighty fallen!'

Craig entered to hear the final words. He questioned Coral with his eyes, and she filled in the details. He clearly did not find it amusing.

'That's the reputation he has. Didn't you know?' His mouth was pulled in with distaste. Marius shook his head.

'As a matter of fact, I didn't. Where did you hear it?'

Craig shrugged. 'In the wind! I thought it was generally known. Women can't keep their hands off him.'

'So I have just seen. Well, I just hope he can keep her under control.'

'You're not having dinner with them?' Coral asked. He shook his head and came near to grinning.

'No. I offered! I suggested that Alicia and I should meet them at eight in the Peacock Room. But she said,' (he stood up and minced effeminately around the desk), '"Piers and me's going to take advantage of room service. We've got a lot of jet-lag to get over, haven't we, Piers darling?"' He snorted. 'Jet-lag! All I hope is he'll be fit to play when she's finished with him.' He swung round to Craig. 'He's not young, you know.' He poked his administrative officer in the chest. 'I think I'll turn *you* loose on her. Release you for special service.'

He was wickedly amused to see Craig's face pale, and a look of anguish flicker in his eyes.

'I'd rather have nothing to do with either of them,' Craig said sharply, turning on his heel and leaving.

Coral put her hand over her mouth. 'You've upset him!'

'I wasn't serious. I don't throw people to the lions—well, more of a tiger, really.'

'Is she really awful?' Coral said, giggling suddenly. 'I mean, *really*?'

'She can't be that bad,' Alicia said. 'Surely?'

'She's the modern equivalent of the meeting of east and west. In her case, the East End of London and the West Indies! The new Britisher.'

'You're racist.'

'I'm cross. I've waited for this moment for two years. Then Ligorno—well, *that* happened. But I thought, well, Alessandri's coming, and life goes on and all that. And then this.'

'Poor Marius! What a pity we're not dining with them. I might have enjoyed it.'

He picked at the food on his plate. 'I've lost the taste for this festival,' he said sadly. 'I feel like a child whose toy has come to pieces in his hand. Who'll put it together for me?'

'It'll look better in the morning. Get an early night.'

'I shan't sleep.' But when she looked in on him before she showered he was breathing like a child, one hand hanging out of bed, as relaxed as a rag doll.

10

Detective-sergeant Verdun sat at his desk, deep in thought. Before him was a pad with notes neatly written, phrases underlined. He stared at them, his eyes sliding slowly down the page. He was looking for a pattern.

'So what have we got?' he asked Briggs, whose notes were not quite so neat, and could only be read by their owner. 'Interpol?'

'Yes.' He turned pages. 'Yes, nothing there about the lady. Clean sheet, they said.'

'Is that all they said?'

Briggs read from his notes. 'No suspicion of any kind of involvement with any of the usual areas of criminality which might conceivably lead to a revenge murder, or a killing to guard secrecy.'

'Did *they* say that?'

'Well, sort of. I put it into better English. The bloke I spoke to was French.'

'Very perspicacious of you, Briggs.'

The constable glanced up suspiciously. 'I thought that was what you'd want.'

'Absolutely. What else did they say?'

'She had no acquaintances or family linked with Mafia business, and no known connections with shady dealings in the drugs world.' He sat back, pleased with himself.

Verdun turned a page of his own notes. He knew that her husband had died ten years earlier; he had also been an upright citizen, Madame's manager before his final illness. There had been no children, simply endless hours of practice, the non-stop tours, audiences, pianos, applause, hotel rooms and concert halls in one great kaleidoscope of colour and sound. And it seemed that her visit to Australia would reveal no kind of aberrant behaviour—except that someone had killed her.

The notes on the page were reminders to him of the personalities involved in the case. In his own mind he discounted the possibility that any members of the hotel staff—or any casual passer-by—had gone to the room and shot Ligorno.

'It's puzzling,' he said to Briggs. 'Nothing had been taken; no assault had accompanied the shooting. No one had been searching for anything, I'd swear to that. So what was it about?' He revisited the murder scene in his mind. 'It's a narrow entry to the room, just door width, with the bathroom on one side and a large built-in wardrobe on the other. Well, you've seen it. When she fell, the dress she wore to the concert—a very full skirt, fine rose-coloured velvet—spread out all across the floor. Carnations and roses scattered everywhere.

'Nothing was marked, was it? That velvet would have shown a footmark. Or flowers would have been crushed if someone had tried to step across. And her foot fell against the door—well, we had a job opening it, didn't we? I don't see how anyone could have entered that room. She was guarding it!'

'Couldn't she have invited the murderer in, and been shot when he was leaving?'

'No! He had those flowers in his hands. If he had taken them in he would have given them to her, wouldn't he? She would have put them down somewhere. But she didn't hold them—she *grabbed* them. You saw the little cuts in her fingers, and thorns embedded. She grabbed them as she went down.'

He could see it clearly in imagination. The knock on the door, the door opening, the flowers, the shot, the falling—the door closing quickly, assisted by Madame's foot, which then had stiffened in its out-thrust position and given them a hard time entering.

'I can see *how*,' he said. 'But I can't see why. We need a really juicy clue. Otherwise I can see big difficulties with this case. And that, Briggs, makes me angry!'

'I'm going to see this policeman feller,' Sir Beverly yelled down the phone. 'Want to come, Clarissa?'

'There's absolutely no need to shout, Beverly. I'm not deaf, even if you are.' She glanced down at her diary, open on the desk. 'When are you going? I'm free at eleven.' She held the receiver away from her ear with an expression of distaste.

'I'll be free at eleven,' he said, as if she hadn't spoken. 'Want to come?'

'What's it for?' She sighed. Why he used the phone was a mystery to her. 'What's—it—for?' she said, loudly and very precisely.

'Got to ginger these people up! Need a boot behind them. Nothing'll get done if we don't give it a good hard shove in the ar...'

'That'll be quite enough, Beverly,' she said in her most penetrating voice. '*Quite* enough! You can pick me up here. I shall be ready.'

'I'll pick you up there.' he roared. 'Be ready!'

Dame Clarissa put the phone down slowly. Beverly wouldn't get anywhere. He never did these days. People saw him coming—heard him, most likely—and ran a mile. He was a silly old coot, but in her way she was rather fond of him. They were two of a kind, left over from some more gracious age when it was all right to wear gloves and a hat, be seen in the right places, know the right people. She could sympathise with him in a way, because she, too, felt as if she were acting in the wrong play. There was no place for them in the socialist world they had inherited after the war. Lady Bountiful was an anachronism in the welfare state, and just what her role in life was she no longer knew.

'To get out and leave it to the young ones,' she told herself, going to her bedroom to change into something more suitable for interviewing a police officer. Or being interviewed by him. She chose a navy blue dress with ecru collar and cuffs, and moved everything out of the handbag she had been using into one that matched. As she turned from the mirror she caught a glimpse of herself, and paused, regarding her image with sharp, unyielding eyes.

'You're old, Clarissa,' she said, and the pale figure stared back at her with a trace of malevolence. 'The passions are over, and it's all downhill to the cemetery from now on.'

As she waited for Beverly to arrive she wondered idly who would mourn her. Few, she suspected. But she hoped, she hoped with an old woman's yearning, that Marius Hogbein would be one.

Sir Beverly's Rolls slid to her front steps, and he blew a blast on the horn. Clarissa took a deep, steadying breath. She would have to listen to bellowing, hectoring and bombast; but she might find out something, anything, and perhaps she could protect that nice Nick Verdun from the worst of the old man's savagery. She walked out (deliberately slow, let him wait for her). Beverly was leaning out of the window.

'Come on, old girl! How long does it take to get you moving? I'm going to show that young man a thing or two. Time he got this case wrapped up. Needs a good kick to get started!'

'And who's going to administer this kick?' Dame Clarissa asked sarcastically. 'You? You couldn't stand on one foot to deliver it, Beverly. Don't talk arrant nonsense!' She sat upright, staring out of the window as they moved in stately fashion down the drive and out into traffic which parted respectfully for them when it became clear that he had no intention of stopping. 'If you intended killing us, you silly man, you should have done it at home and saved the car!'

Sir Beverly leaned out of the window to berate a lesser mortal. 'That told him a thing or two!' he said with satisfaction, narrowly missing a bus. 'The roads are full of fools and knaves. Government ought to do something about it.'

'You are an impossibly stupid old man,' Dame Clarissa said; but she said it quietly so that his deaf old ears should not hear it. For they *were* two of a kind, and she *was* fond of him in an exasperated sort of way; and if they didn't stick together, what hope was there for them?

'So what's going on?' Sir Beverly demanded in tones that could be heard all over police headquarters. 'What progress have you made? Are we any nearer to a solution?'

Verdun leaned back in his chair, calling up all his reserves of patience. 'Now, Sir Beverly,' he said calmly, 'you know I couldn't tell you—not even you,' he concluded, hoping the small sop would work. It didn't.

'That means you're no forrarder! As I thought. Always ready to proclaim your successes, you chappies. Different matter when it's a failure. No leaping for publicity then.'

'You'd hardly expect it, would you?' Verdun said reasonably. 'We're not going to tell the crims out there that they're winning. You wouldn't want us to, would you?'

'So there's no progress.' He turned to Dame Clarissa. 'Much as I expected.'

'You have to be patient, Beverly. I'm sure Sergeant Verdun is doing everything in his power. He certainly doesn't want murderers running around on the loose.' She smiled encouragingly—'like a shark before the bite,' Verdun told himself. 'The festival couldn't stand any more scandals.'

Verdun leaned forward. 'I don't think there's any fear of a repeat performance. This seems a peculiarly meaningless crime, and hardly likely to recur.' He placed his hands together and regarded his broad fingers absently. 'There is no motive that anyone can discover—and we have been in touch with Interpol, Sir Beverly. They can find no background for a crime of this sort.'

'Feller must have been mad, then!' The old man leaned forward, preparing to struggle to his feet. 'Can't legislate for madness, I suppose. Just thought he'd kill someone. Or perhaps he objected to the way the lady used the loud pedal.' He gave a tempestuous bellow of laughter. 'Perhaps it was that clot Hal—Hal—critic chappie. Just the sort of thing a half-sloshed critic might do, eh?' He dug Verdun in the shoulder. 'Eh? Eh?' He turned, one finger extended to poke Dame Clarissa; but at the icy look in her cold grey eyes he stopped, blowing a walrus-snort that was the nearest he ever got to embarrassment.

'I hope you won't repeat that, Sir Beverly,' Verdun said with real solemnity. 'If Mr Princeton heard it he would be within his rights to take action.'

'That twerp? Against me?' Sir Beverly humphed, but he subsided, settling back into his chair with a disgruntled air. Clarissa took her chance.

'Mr Verdun—is it possible that Camille Ligorno should have been the cause of—well, jealousy? A broken love affair, for example. Someone who had been in some way *damaged* by her undoubted successes? Jealousy is a very strong emotion, after all.'

'I would like to think you're right, Dame Clarissa,' the detective said, relieved to be faced with a more rational interrogator. 'But there simply is no evidence pointing that way, at least so far.'

'So this is likely to go down as an unsolved mystery? A blot on the escutcheon of our police force? A failure by our festival to protect its own?' She sighed deeply. 'This will go hard with poor Mr Hogbein,' she said in tones of lamentation.

'It will go hard with me!' Verdun said, pushing back his chair. 'And I should remind you that it is still only a matter of hours since the lady was killed. It's only on TV that crimes get solved in a couple of hours. There's work to be done.'

'Of course,' she said gently. She held out her hand to him and he shook it gravely. 'Come on, Beverly!' She patted the old man on the arm, and together they left the room, Verdun staring after them, seeing two people out of their time, as pointless as nosebags on a space ship.

'Poor old devils!' he muttered, and got back to reality.

Sir Beverly crashed his gears into reverse and barely scraped past a police van. 'These bloody fellers don't know how to park!' he ground through clamped teeth, flinging the gear lever forward and making a series of erratic jumps.

Dame Clarissa hung on to the door handle. 'If you intend committing suicide, kindly allow me to alight and call a taxi! I have not lived this long in order to be cut bleeding from your Rolls-Royce.'

'Damned fuss about nothing!' he swore at her. 'Never had an accident. Don't know what you're talking about.' At that moment the ugly sound of tearing metal was heard from somewhere behind them, and the car came to unscheduled halt. Dame Clarissa opened the door and climbed out. With splendid command of herself she walked past a Mercedes, whose immaculate wing was now entangled with the Rolls' back bumper, and stalked into the foyer of the police station.

'Kindly call me a taxi!' she ordered the young policewoman on the desk; and she, cowed by Clarissa's eight decades of getting her own way, did as she was bid.

11

A pain he might be, an insufferable egotist tramping through all Marius's careful planning, but one thing was certain. Away from the sultry Tabitha and seated before a fine piano, Piers Alessandri was superb.

Marius watched him from the back of the King's Hall as he rehearsed, meticulously repeating a phrase that failed to please him, sometimes standing and listening to the reverberations of what all agreed was a fine concert venue. Tabitha had been packed off with a purse full of money, and told not to return until dinner-time; and the ban had not appeared to upset her.

'I was afraid,' Marius said to Coral, 'that she would get in the way. But he seems to have her measure.'

'She's a clothes-horse,' Coral said shortly. 'She's a spender. She knows that if she gets in his way the goodies will stop. There are rules in that game, you know.'

'It's not a world I know much about—the kept woman,' he said mildly. 'I'm just thankful he hasn't lost all his marbles.'

'It's not his marbles he should lose,' Coral said darkly, blushing slightly. Marius glanced at her curiously. 'His eyes are everywhere,' she explained defiantly. 'You'd think one at a time would be enough. But he's got to spread it all about. Gwenny's bowled over by him.' Gwenny was the girl on the switchboard.

'Gwenny's in a perpetual state of being bowled over,' Marius said unkindly. 'Look at how she was with the Filthy Seven last year!'

'Well, they were rather special—all that sex appeal!'

'And not much musicianship. I was sold a pup on that one.'

'Who needs musicianship when they've got—IT?' Coral rolled her eyes at him. 'Musicianship is the refuge of the sexual failure.'

Marius snorted. 'Try telling that to Alessandri!'

'Only joking.' Suddenly she sat down, her face crumpling. 'Oh God, I wish they'd find out who did it.' Marius nodded dismally.

'It's suffocating. Chin up—only another week and the festival will be over and we can begin to think again. It's tragic, I know, but we have to get used to it. Ligorno's gone.' They were silent. 'And Alessandri is sounding divine. Tomorrow should be a triumph, all round.'

Coral blew her nose. 'Does *she* want a ticket?'

He gave a swift smile. 'Apparently not. Alessandri said, "Tabitha's interests lie elsewhere".' He gave a very fair imitation of the pianist's Italian accent.

'Where, I wonder?' Coral said, sniffing.

'Ah! I wasn't game to ask.'

At the afternoon rehearsal the rapport between the conductor, Vlad Koblenz, and the distinguished Italian performer was instantaneous. Marius listened to half of the Brahms' First and knew that it was going to be true high-spot of the festival's music. He went home, hoping that Alicia would be there; he was in need of a cup of good tea and some consolation. He could imagine that he would carry the scars of the past few days for the rest of his life.

According to her diary, Alicia was at a meeting in Dame Clarissa's house, planning fund-raising for the next year's festivities. He pulled a face; far be it from him to complain at their earnest enthusiasm, but he couldn't even begin to think about the future. He boiled the kettle and was burning some toast when she came home, cool and attractive in creamy yellow with gold-trimmed sandals. He put his arms around her.

'You look like an ice-lolly,' he whispered. 'Let me lick you!'

'Put me down,' she said calmly. 'You don't know where I've been.'

He sat on a kitchen stool and watched her. 'I do. I looked in your diary. The old dame's place.'

'Don't be disrespectful. She does a lot for you.' She made the tea. 'Come into the other room. It's cooler.'

They drank, companionably silent. After a while he said, 'If it *was* someone involved with the festival…'

Alicia shook her head. 'Let it go. If it is, we shall know soon enough. If not, it simply makes it hard to go on.'

'I need to know,' he said simply, and she looked across at him.

'I know you do. But you'll go mad if you try to take that on as well as everything else.'

'You're a wise woman, Alicia.'

She smiled. 'I know. It's one of my things.'

'I'm so lucky.'

'You certainly are. You could have been trapped by a little Tabitha, and then where would you be?'

'Don't even joke about it!' he said wrathfully. 'That woman is poison.'

Alicia laughed suddenly. 'I know! I saw here this morning, out shopping. She had someone trotting behind her, carrying her loot, like in one of those old Hollywood films. I should think she's spent his fee already.'

'Just let it get over,' Marius said, finishing his tea. 'Just get it over and get them out! I need a break.'

There was a buzz of excitement in the King's Hall. This was what people had been waiting for—a musical giant playing music fit for his stature. Ligorno had been great, but Bach wasn't for everyone. The big orchestra, the big sound was what turned people on.

Craig Schuster and Jim Fletcher stood at the back of the balcony, looking down on the panorama of heads, the entrepreneur's dream, a packed house.

'There's nothing quite like it,' Jim said. 'The sense of anticipation. The electricity! I've only heard him on disc. It'll be a terrific experience.'

Craig, abstracted, unexpectedly said, 'I saw him in the States. He's certainly got something.' He was grudging.

Marius joined Alicia in their seats, and looked around him with restored pleasure. 'You can't beat it, can you?' He took her hand. 'Thank you!'

'For what?'

'For being there.'

A mighty programme: late Beethoven to start and Mahler to finish. And set in the centre a jewel! Marius sat back and prepared to let the stresses go. In a seat towards the rear Verdun sat, melting into the audience and not missing a thing. Coral scurried about backstage, then slipped round to the front and took her seat. Mave Cardwell checked her ticket against her seat number—she didn't always go to concerts, but she felt that this was different. Two rows behind, Hal Princeton sat with notebook at the ready, waiting for what he truly hoped would be a sublime experience.

And so it proved to be. It was one of those special occasions that would be remembered down the years, against which other similar occasions would be measured. The music seemed to light up the hall; a tremendous unity born of the love of the music and discipline and the highest order of musicianship carried audience, performers, even backstage staff up into an experience that few had ever felt before.

During ecstatic applause, while Alessandri and Koblenz and the orchestra stood in silent, drained acknowledgement of their achievement, Marius slipped out and was waiting when Alessandri appeared, sweat running down his face, in the dressing room. Marius took his hand in silent adoration of the wonderful gift he had just witnessed. 'Stunning!' he said humbly. 'We shall never forget it.'

Alessandri bent graciously from a great height. 'It is my pleasure!' For a moment there was nothing between them but sincerity and admiration. Then, as a crowd started to gather outside the room, Alessandri began to remove his soaked collar.

'I change now. I go back to the hotel. I can do ten autographs, no more. Please to tell them.'

Marius returned to earth with a bump. For a moment he was struck dumb. 'But...' he began

'It is not good to be seen too much,' Alessandri said kindly. 'It destroys the image.' Marius backed away, nodding stupidly. 'There is no value in an autograph if everyone has one. Is this not so?'

Outside, Marius faced the eager throng. 'Mr Alessandri is very tired, as you can imagine. He will do ten autographs, no more.' In a moment of inspiration he said, 'His hands, of course. We must not ask him...'

Privately, he was seething; but in apparent good humour he took ten programmes and shrugged helplessly at those who had missed out. He opened the door and waited while the indecipherable signature was appended, then handed them back. He remembered Ligorno, gracious, generous, and thought how unfair it was.

'What did you think?' Mave Cardwell said to Hal Princeton as they met in the bar during the interval. There was a crush of people, and they retired to a corner. Hal waved his hands in a gesture of speechless emotion.

'Words!' he said. 'How can I express it in mere words? It was pure magic. Pure enchantment.' Mave nodded, pleased. She had enjoyed it, and hoped she had done so with good reason. 'There comes a time in the life of a critic...' He stopped. 'I am thankful I was spared to hear him,' he said with a kind of dreadful humility.

'That good?' Mave said. 'Very enjoyable, certainly. But *that* good? You must have heard better.'

'I would have remembered anything better than that.' Hal seemed near to tears.

'Are you all right, old dear? Not been drinking on the job, have you?'

He stared at her with unassailable dignity. 'You know I never drink before a concert,' he said, stiffly offended. 'If, out of my wealth of experience, I say that this was something straight out of heaven, why should you doubt my word?'

She hastily refuted the idea. 'If you thought it was that good, who am I to argue.'

When the bells rang for the second half they wandered back together into the auditorium 'I never thought I would find Mahler an anti-climax,' Hal said pensively. 'I almost wish I could go home now and not let the taste of Brahms and Alessandri be tainted by the lesser beauties of the good Gustav. But I shall sit through it. Uncomplaining.' He sighed deeply.

'I'm sure your editor will be very grateful to you,' she said sharply. He wasn't looking at all well. But it was his own choice to drink himself silly, and she'd finished with interfering. She sat down to listen to the final work, less entranced this time because she had started worrying about Hal, and then found herself worrying about the murder. With an effort she dragged her thoughts away from the sordid realities, and tried to lose herself in a musician's fantasy world.

Meanwhile, Alessandri was speeding back to his hotel and the delights of his 'kitten'. Marius, irritated though he was, took comfort in the thought that his episode with the great man was now concluded, apart from the niceties of farewell. It would be a pleasure to see them off for their flight to New Zealand and the next round of concerts; 'and good luck to the Kiwis!' Marius muttered with unexpected venom. 'I hope they enjoy it.'

Mahler came to an end and Koblenz bowed and bowed again, and then it was all over for another night. There was a well-defined feeling that the festival was drawing to its close, a sigh of relief from the faithful that in a few more days they could relax, stay at home in the evening with slippers, a can of beer over the barbie; slip back into sporadic concert-going until the next cultural feast was unleashed in the following year.

('Would they even miss it?' Marius had sometimes asked himself viciously. 'If the festival simply never happened again, would they care?' In which he was less than fair to his devoted audiences.)

Mave took Hal's bony arm and they walked together out into the warm night. 'Look at the stars!' she exclaimed as they paced slowly through the home-going throng. 'What a night it's been.'

'It is given only rarely to a critic to use every superlative in his vocabulary...' Hal said thoughtfully.

'What?'

'The opening of my critique, I think. I shall paint it in warm colours, in golds and crimsons and sunset peach.'

'Very nice! You've really fallen for the old boy, haven't you?'

'Don't be vulgar.'

'He's a bit of a swine, you know,' Mave said wickedly. 'Women! Wine, women and—piano, so I've heard. Got a little bit of stuff tucked away at the hotel.'

'Where,' said Hal, disgusted, 'do you find your squalid pieces of gossip?'

Mave laughed. 'I got this one from Marius, if you must know.'

Hal was silent. 'I don't think,' he said at last, 'that his private morals make any difference. To his immortal soul, perhaps. But not to his status as a musician. It may be the thing that lifts him above the world and opens him to influences that we lesser mortals never experience. I shall pretend I didn't hear you.'

Mave patted his arm. 'My car's here. See you later. I'll look forward to reading your review.'

'Do you think I could use the word "perfection"?' Hal said.

12

'...*to use every superlative in his vocabulary*...' Hal wrote. He sat back in his chair and let the evening wash over him again. Because it was a Saturday night he could take his time about writing his piece; there would be nobody at the newspaper office at this hour. He stood up and wandered about the room, as restless as a teenager in love. The Brahms—the *interpretation* of the Brahms, he corrected himself—had bitten into his soul. He found himself thinking about a time, long ago, when he had hoped that his future was to be found on the concert platform.

He remembered studying that very concerto; he could recall his teacher standing by the window, listening to him, saying warm, exciting things that now he couldn't quite remember, but which then had meant the world.

'Put your life into it, Hal!' Hadn't someone said that? 'Put your life and heart and soul into it, and all your experience, and you will be a fine pianist.'

Then Korea, and the disorientation he had never quite got over, and nothing in his fingers, nothing at all, no sensation of the love he had once felt for those ivory keys. Nothing!

He put his head down on his cold hands, suddenly weary. He would write the thing tomorrow. Let the glory die slowly in his head; let him lie here and try not to remember. Without warning, hot tears began to slide through his fingers. They should have killed him there on the battlefield, quickly. This slow agony was too cruel, even for war. He put out a hand to the bottle that was never far from him. If he slept tonight he might feel better in the morning.

'A message from Signor Alessandri, Marius,' Coral said. 'He would like to spend a couple of hours practising for his New Zealand concerts. Can we find him a piano?'

Marius groaned. He had just had a telegram saying that a band of acrobats had been delayed in Penang, and would have to miss their first performance. 'Give it to Craig,' he said, and shut his door.

Craig scowled. 'Can't Jim? I've got a pile of things to do.'

'Jim's busy,' she said shortly. 'Just ring around. You don't have to take him.'

The recital room behind the King's Hall was vacant, and the manager agreed to open it up for Alessandri. Craig rang the hotel and passed on the message to Tabitha, the very private secretary. He arranged for a car to take the great man to the hall. 'Have I done enough?' he said pointedly to Coral, and she grinned at him.

'More than! When are you going to lunch?'

He glanced at his watch. 'Early. I've got things to do this afternoon.' He stopped at the door. 'If you see Zacaria, tell him I'll be in about two.'

There was peace in the office. Everyone was either busy or out, and Coral took a break and made herself a cup of coffee. It had been a good concert. Marius had been pleased, she knew. Somehow it had made up for the awfulness of the other time, when all the euphoria had disappeared under the stress of Ligorno's murder. She picked up a magazine. They had thought they would never get over it, she thought ruefully; and yet here they were, only few days later, able to enjoy life as if nothing had happened. It was gruesome.

Marius came through her room. 'I'll be out for a while,' he said, and left. She put her feet on the waste paper basket and began to read.

Alessandri came to the end of a Chopin sonata and dropped his hands from the keys. He had sometimes wondered how long he could go on performing, before the inevitable signs began—the critics, the audiences, saying, 'Ah, you should have heard him twenty years ago! *Then* he was a pianist.' But he had heard none of that last night. The applause had been as overwhelming as ever: he had to admit, for sheep farmers they had good taste! He knew he had played superlatively well, that there had been some chemistry between him and Koblenz, some magic which had transmitted itself to the listeners.

He stretched his arms. When he got back to Europe he would pay off his little kitten. He was in the mood for something with more subtlety, more sophistication. It had been fun, rejuvenating in a way; but he always knew when it had to stop. And he rather thought Tabitha did, too, from the way she had been spending his money!

He decided to play one more piece, perhaps some Schumann. When a door opened he took no notice. The manager had told him he could stay until one, if he wished. But when he looked up, his heart contracted with shock. Behind the pistol pointed at his chest were eyes that bored into him relentlessly, coldly; and he knew that he had met the end of his career.

'No, wait! There is some mistake!'

'No mistake.' The voice was soft, almost gentle. 'This is for Melanie. Do you remember Melanie?'

'No—no! I never knew anyone of that name.'

'You're a liar! A good pianist, but a bad liar.'

'Don't do that!' Alessandri said. He was determined not to beg. 'It will be an unforgivable crime.'

'Well—you should know about that.'

There was a terrible pause, as if there was something still to say. 'Melanie?' asked Piers Alessandri, and died.

He toppled slowly from the stool, and the assassin stood for a moment and then turned and left the hall. There was no one to see. No one would come near. Last movement! Coda! Finale! No *da capo* repeat for the famous—no, the late—Alessandri.

13

Verdun returned from his lunch and sat at his desk, staring morosely at the file marked 'LIGORNO: Madame Camille.' It was a symbol of failure for him, a nagging ache. It seemed absurd that a murder could be committed so simply, and yet defy solution.

He leaned across wearily when the phone rang. It was Coral Stone, and he didn't need to be unduly sensitive to know that she was close to hysteria.

'Please—take it slowly! What's happened?'

Coral closed her eyes and took a deep breath. 'They've just found Signor Alessandri—please come quickly!'

'Found him?' He stood up hastily. 'Found him where?'

'Someone's sh-shot him!' Coral said, breaking down. 'In the recital room. Oh, please come quickly...'

He grabbed his bag, shouting for Briggs as he ran out of the room. Together they arrived at the hall, and he broke through the little knot of people at the door. The manager, white-faced, took him inside and closed the door behind them.

'He'd been here since about eleven. Practising—for New Zealand. And we went for lunch about twelve, and came back about one-fifteen. There was nothing to do here, you understand. No concerts until next week.'

They were standing together, looking down on the mortal remains of the great man. Even in death he managed to look elegant, though the silver hair had been slightly ruffled by his fall. In the centre of his chest was a dark, ugly stain where the life-blood had drained away. Otherwise, he might have been asleep.

'Who found him?' Verdun asked.

'My secretary. She knew he was rehearsing, and when she came back she heard nothing and assumed he had finished and gone. Then, when she crossed the foyer, she saw that the door was slightly open and that there was still a light on. She opened the door and went in, and...' He shrugged, gesturing helplessly towards the dead man. 'She was shattered, of course. I've sent her home. You can see her there—I've got the address.'

'Nothing been moved?'

'No. No one's been let in. My God—what's happening? *Murders—here?* It's inconceivable!'

'Yes.' Verdun walked around the body, looking at it from every angle. 'Briggs, go round the hall and see if there's anything that shouldn't be there. And, Briggs, we shall need to know if it was the same gun. Get on to that, will you?'

Briggs, still not quite used to dead bodies, nodded and went to the back of the room. Verdun glanced at the carpet that stretched from platform to door, and noted entries and exits. The door opened and his team entered, photographer and doctor and two bearing a stretcher. He left them to get on with it.

Marius was in his office by the time Verdun arrived there. 'I knew you'd be coming. Coral told me...' He closed his eyes for a moment, his face white with shock. 'I simply can't believe it, Verdun. What's gone wrong?'

'I wish I knew. Tell me about Alessandri. I know what he was as a musician—I was at the concert last night. But as a man...?'

Marius took a deep breath, his eyes going beyond the detective as if he could see and evaluate the dead man. 'He was not a nice person,' he said at last. 'If I say that for two years I have looked forward to meeting him properly, and after three days I was looking forward to seeing him go—well!' He shrugged.

'What form did it take?'

'Well, he was a ladies' man, I suppose you'd say. He had a little tart here with…My God!' He sat up with a sudden realisation. 'Someone'll have to tell her.'

'We'll do that. Where is she? Name?' He scribbled down a few details. 'A tart, you say?'

'You'll know the moment you see her.' Marius rubbed his hand over his face. 'The repercussions,' he said flatly. 'I daren't think about it.'

'Who knew Alessandri would be there, at the recital room, this afternoon?'

'Anyone. It was no secret.'

'I shall have to see your staff. Give me an hour with the girlfriend, and have everybody back here by—say, four o'clock.' It was a command. The situation had gone beyond friendly relationships; now everyone was suspect. Marius nodded wearily.

'I'll see they're here.'

'What is there on tonight?'

'Festival? Two plays running at two theatres, a film, an outdoor folk festival, a reception for a group of Russian artists—painters— which I ought to be at. That's about all, I think.'

'Carry on as usual. But hold yourself ready. This has put a very different complexion on things.'

Marius watched him leave. His sense of despair was crushing. He lifted the phone. 'Gwenny, get Mrs Hogbein, please.'

But all he got from Gwenny was a series of gulping sobs.

At four Marius's office was full of people. No one spoke, for there was little to say. Worse, it was impossible to meet anyone's eyes, for they were all afraid of what they might see there. One murder, they might have been thinking, could be an aberration; but two…? Someone, perhaps someone in the room, had taken two valuable lives. It was a thought not conducive to conversation.

Verdun came in, moving swiftly, decisively. He took Marius's place at the desk without a by-your-leave, and threw a shrewd glance around him. If they saw a man who spelt danger for them, he saw a montage of white, distraught faces: Coral, clutching a handkerchief; Gwenny, eyes swollen and red; Jim Fletcher, sunk in his chair, barely raising his eyes above the desk top; Craig Schuster, pale, controlled, staring up at the detective with anxious intensity; and Marius himself, perched on a chair against the wall, his nerves in tatters and a rising anger in him that anyone should use his festival for such foully criminal ends.

'Anyone else?' Verdun asked.

'These are the people who in some way had to deal with Signor Alessandri. There are a couple of typists, one or two others who have no part in the main activities of the festival. And, of course, people at the recital room.'

'I'll see them later. So—we'll start.' He took a moment to order his thoughts. 'You are all aware of what has happened. This murder seems a reasonable copy of the other. Mme Ligorno also was shot without fuss, no struggle, neat and tidy, no witnesses. This is why I must speak to you, separately and together. First, who knew that Alessandri was going to the recital room to practise?'

Slowly, unwillingly, hands went up. 'I knew,' said Marius. 'I left it to Craig to organise.'

'I rang the manager, made the arrangements, called for a taxi to the hall—and then went and had lunch.' Craig glanced around him. 'It was all done on the phone.'

Briggs was scribbling in his notebook. He looked up as Coral spoke.

'I heard him.'

Verdun turned to Jim, who jumped slightly and mopped his face. 'I was working. In my office. I didn't hear anything until Coral told me—what had happened...' He tailed off, looking round for confirmation. But no one had eyes for him.

Gwenny suddenly emitted a sob. 'Oh, dear, I'm sorry! I'm really sorry! He was such a lovely man.' She put out a hand to Coral. 'I know I'm being silly, Coral—but he *was* lovely.' Coral patted her hand and turned to Verdun.

'Can Gwenny go? She doesn't know anything about this.' Verdun regarded the girl for a moment, then nodded. Gwenny left, sniffing miserably.

Private interviews revealed nothing more. The sense of gloom that lay over everything inhibited normal work, and when they left to go home they took with them deep and fearful emotions. For while once might be an isolated incident, twice opened a can of worms into which they preferred not to look. Who might be next?

Marius opened his front door—and Alicia was not there! If he had ever needed a pair of arms around him, now was the time. He wandered out onto the terrace and stood looking over the garden, seeing nothing. A sense of horror had gripped him; that anyone could do such a thing passed his understanding. His festival, the great and wondrous burden that he carried year in and year out, was doomed. Who would want to perform in the future if the fee included a bullet? He could see a world-wide ban on him; if he left here, would anyone else ever employ him? He doubted it.

The phone rang and he went inside to answer it, dreading what it might be. It was Mave Cardwell. 'I rang Carol about some tickets,' she said, 'and she told me. Good God, Marius, what's happening to us?' The suppressed glee she had once displayed had quite gone.

He answered as well as he could; and then it was Dame Clarissa, followed in quick succession by a rampant Sir Beverly and an anguished, despairing Hal Princeton.

At that moment Alicia came in, took the phone from him and replaced it, then held out her arms. 'Marius…Marius…' she murmured. 'It's not your fault! Here, let me get you a drink.'

'Where did you hear?'

'I rang to speak to you. Coral was just leaving—she told me.' She watched him carefully; slowly, colour returned to his ashen cheeks.

'It's the end, you know. After all these years…'

'Nonsense!' she said vigorously. 'It's a passing tragedy. You'll see.' She sipped her own drink, then had a thought. 'Has anyone told Tiger-Kitten?'

'Verdun. He wanted to. No one else did.'

Alicia gave a tiny smile. 'Lucky man!'

Tabitha opened her door and she was pouting. When she saw it was Nick Verdun the pout slipped out of sight and became a seductive smile. He stepped forward.

'May I come in?'

She held the door wide. 'If you want. There's only me here.'

'It was you I wanted to see.'

She showed no surprise; Verdun, watching her carefully, felt this would be her normal attitude. She expected men to want to see her.

'Sit down,' she said in a voice that still bore the speech patterns of Brixton while assuming a velvety quality that he felt sure would slip under pressure. He was right; when he gave her the tragic news she was silent for a long, paralysed moment; then she flung herself back in the chair and drummed her hands on its arms.

'I don't believe you!' she screamed. ''ow could 'e be dead? 'e was 'ere only a bit ago! Crikey, 'e was right 'ere!' She pointed dramatically to a pattern in the carpet. 'What 'appened to 'im, then, eh? 'eart attack, was it? I told 'im 'e was overdoin' it—at 'is age! Too much for an old man, it was. What 'appened to 'im?'

Verdun kept his eyes on her. 'He was shot. Murdered. Like Mme Ligorno. I'm sorry.'

The dark skin lost its glow. 'Oh, gawd!' she whispered. 'Oh, gor-blimey! Piers—murdered? Why?'

'It would help us if we knew.' He took out his notebook, flipped it open. 'Where have you been since, say, eleven this morning?'

'Me?' She sat upright, shocked. ''ere, you don't think it was me, do you?'

Verdun held her eyes with his own steady gaze. 'I have no opinions at this stage. I simply want facts.'

'Was it—somethink to do with that other—Ligorno?'

'Facts.' He said, calmly but with determination.

''cos if it was, that lets me out. We wasn't even 'ere.' She stared at him with a flicker of triumph.

'That's no defence. There have been copy-cat murders before. Where were you?'

She regarded him with a look in which momentary panic had been replaced by natural cunning. 'Out—shopping!' She indicated a pile of carrier bags and boxes. 'Out for lunch...'

'When?'

'About—oh, half-twelve.'

'Where?'

She mentioned an expensive restaurant. 'They'd remember me.'

'I'm sure they would.'

She gave him a swift grin of acknowledgment. 'Then back 'ere. Tryin' on the gear.'

He looked down at his notes. 'So, during the whole period you were within, say, ten minutes of the recital room. Ten minutes on foot.'

'I don't go *on foot*!' She was scornfully amused.

'Five minutes, then. In a taxi?'

'What do you mean?'

'Did you hire a taxi?'

She glared at him. 'Yes, I did. But not to go to no toffee-nosed recital room. Why would I?'

He frowned, slightly watching her. 'Perhaps Signor Alessandri had begun to tire of you? That would be a reason for shooting him.' He glanced round the room. 'Plenty to lose!'

'Him? Tire of me?' She was getting her nerve, and her aitches, back. 'Not that way round, brother! No one ditches me. I was going to—review the situation when we got back to Europe. All that bloody music—bo-*ring!*'

'So perhaps he wasn't prepared to lose you? Maybe you couldn't get rid of him.'

'Listen, I'm good at this game. I been doin' it since I was a kid. There's always a right time—to start, to stop. An' the right time was comin' up. For me! For him, too, maybe. Nothin's for ever, man. Is it?' She stood up, smoothing her skirt down over shapely hips. 'It was time to move on.'

'Either way,' Verdun said coolly, putting away his notes, 'you had a motive. Do you have a gun?'

'Do me a favour! What would I want with a gun? It's not the way I work.'

Outside her door Verdun stood for a moment in thought. 'No,' he murmured at last, 'I don't suppose it is.'

14

Craig sat opposite Verdun, his hands loosely clasped, legs crossed at the ankles. He wore an expression of concern, and the detective, regarding him with interest, made a mental note of the combination of relaxation and obvious emotional involvement.

'You movements this morning?' he suggested. 'From, say, the moment when you rang to arrange Alessandri's practice session.'

Craig narrowed his eyes, thinking carefully. 'I had intended to work up to a late lunch. Lots of paperwork.'

'I should have thought that now the festival was ending you would have had considerably less.'

'It looks like it, I know. But. of course, we're dealing with festival planning up to three years ahead. It's long-term work *and* short-term work combined.' He sat himself up in his chair. 'Then, when Marius asked me to organise the recital room, I decided to change my timetable and lunch early then come back and work straight through until the evening. I was going on to the acrobats second show later.'

'Why did you change your mind?'

Craig shrugged. 'I suppose I was irritated. You know how it is—you plan something and then something else crops up? I thought I might get more done if I was back at work by one, and had six straight hours ahead of me.'

Verdun nodded lowly, writing in his neat hand. 'Then? After you had arranged the practice session?'

'I—finished off some letters, I think. Put them in envelopes. Told Coral I was off, put the letters in the mail tray...' His eyes were closed as he visualised his steps. 'Than I walked up to Blenheim Street, where there's a sandwich bar, and bought two packets of sandwiches...' He opened his eyes and caught Verdun's calm gaze. 'Chicken and salad, tuna and gherkin! And a take-away of rather dreadful coffee.'

'Where do you usually lunch?'

'In the café next to the sandwich bar. They do a nice pasta.'

'Why not today?'

For a moment Craig seemed uncomfortable, 'I—I wanted to think. I decided to go down into the Court Lane gardens. I could be alone there.'

'To think about what?' Verdun missed nothing, not a flicker of eyelids, not a flexing of muscle. 'What needed thinking about?'

'Look...' Craig leaned forward. 'If I tell you, don't mention it to Marius. He's got enough at the moment.' Verdun nodded. 'I was wondering if it was time for me to move on. I've enjoyed working here, but I get restless. Recently...'

'Why "recently"?'

Craig looked down at his feet. 'Since I became a widower,' he said in precise, unemotional tones, 'I have found it difficult to stay in one place for long.'

Verdun surveyed him thoughtfully. 'You wife died—when?'

'A few years ago.'

'How did she die?'

There was a long pause. 'She was driving home—late at night—took a wrong turning—drove over a steep drop. She was killed outright.'

'I'm sorry. Where was this—Australia?'

'No—oh, no, we were in America. California. I waited half the night—a flat tyre, I thought—then I rang the police. And... they found her.' He closed his eyes. 'The car had caught fire. They wouldn't let me see her.'

'I'm sorry,' Verdun said again, with obvious sincerity. 'Could you, perhaps, give me the date of her death?'

Craig looked sharply at him. 'I don't see why I should.'

'In a case of double murder I must have every bit of information I can find. You can see that, I'm sure. To disprove as much as to prove. To eliminate, perhaps. The more detailed the picture, the sooner it makes sense.'

Craig held the gaze for a moment, then relaxed. He gave the information, if not willingly, at least without argument.

'Now,' Verdun said, letting the old tragedy go, 'whereabouts in the gardens did you sit?' Craig described a secluded spot. 'And you were there—how long?'

'About thirty-five, forty minutes, I suppose.'

'And did anyone see you?' He shot a piercing glance at Craig, who shook his head slowly.

'I shouldn't think so. Because I didn't want to be disturbed.' He seemed to have gained some buoyancy, allowing a glimmer of dry humour to appear. 'No alibi, I'm afraid! The sandwich bar *might* remember me, but that's not what you're looking for, is it? When do you reckon the—he was killed?'

'By about twelve-thirty, probably. Can't be more precise.'

'Well, I can't offer you anything. I was under a tree, well-hidden from the footpath, and I don't remember seeing anyone who would have noticed me.'

Verdun closed his book. 'Thank you, Mr Schuster.' Craig stood, moving his shoulders as if they were stiff. He nodded to Verdun and made his way to the door. 'By the way, do you have a gun?'

Craig stopped and turned. 'A gun?'

'Yes—a gun. Medium calibre. Fitted with a silencer.'

'No, I don't!' He gave a short laugh devoid of humour. 'Not even in the States, where everyone has one.' At the door he stopped. 'And at this moment in time, if I did have such a thing I don't think I would be telling you.'

'Probably not. We shall be testing for gun residue, powder and so on, this afternoon.'

Craig gave a brief nod and left.

Verdun remained standing with his eyes on the door after it closed. He was sensing Craig Schuster's aura, his personality, his emotional 'field', as an animal sniffs the air for invisible information.

'I demand,' Sir Beverly was saying in a kind of bovine tantrum, 'I *demand* to see this feller whatsisname—Vardon!' He stood, legs sturdily planted, in front of the reception desk, and biffed it with his clenched fist.

'Detective-Sergeant Verdun,' the young constable said bravely, 'is occupied. If you will give me your name...'

'Give you my name?' exploded Sir Beverly, as touchy as a duellist. 'What d'you mean—give you my name? You *know* who I am!'

'I'm sorry, sir. I'm new here. Your name, please.'

At that moment, Craig Schuster emerged from his interrogation, and the old knight blustered over to him.

'You been in there, have you, with this policeman chappie?'

But Craig did not stop. His eyes passed over Sir Beverly and appeared not to recognise him. The old man, taken aback, watched him go out of the foyer into sunlight, then turned to face Verdun's door. Irate, bristling, he plunged towards it.

'You can't go in there, sir!' cried the constable, but that was not language comprehensible to Sir Beverly. He flung the door open and faced a solemn, contemplative Nick Verdun, whose sigh of exasperation was quite lost in his visitor's fulminations. Verdun nodded reassuringly to the discomfited constable.

'Now, Sir Beverly,' he said loudly, closing the door, 'what can I do for you?'

'You can tell me what's going on, young man! Damned wops getting themselves killed all over the place. Lowers the tone! What are you doing about it—hey? Hey?'

Verdun bored into him with a coldly authoritative stare. It was all he could think of on the spur of the moment. 'We are pursuing our enquiries...' he began.

'Pursuing—bulldust! People being shot, right, left and centre—something's got to be done.'

'Something *is* being done.' Verdun produced his voice to pierce the deaf ears and impenetrable egotism of his adversary. '*We—are—pursuing—the—usual...*'

'You are pursuing nothing!' Sir Beverly said rudely. 'What about interrogation? Grilling? Third degree? Offering a reward! Eh?'

'Are *you* offering a reward?' Verdun felt himself growing angry, and relaxed deliberately. 'Sir Beverly, I am interrogating—*in my own way*—everybody who may be involved in Signor Alessandri's murder. I would have got round to you this evening. You have saved me the trouble. *Where were you at lunchtime today?*'

There was a dead (and welcome) silence for a long moment. Sir Beverly, it seemed, did not believe his ears. 'Me?' he said, outraged. 'Me? You're going to interrogate *me?*'

'Everyone!' said Verdun with satisfaction. It was not given to many to silence Sir Beverly Stainer.

'What's the matter, Jim?' Coral said, as he wandered aimlessly through her office for the umpteenth time. Jim put his hands in his jeans pockets and hunched his shoulders as if he felt cold.

'Nothing—nothing! Can't settle.'

'I know. It's ghastly, isn't it? I wonder what...' She stopped suddenly, and it was plain to both of them that this was not the time of the place to share confidences.

'It's getting to us, isn't it?' Jim said morosely. 'Now that we're all suspects...'

'Are we?'

'Aren't we?' He looked out of the window. 'Funny! Out there nothing's changed. Sails on the water, blue skies, sunshine—but in here it's gone dark.' Coral watched him, wanting to feel sympathetic; but prevented by the knowledge that any form of depression or neurotic instability might indicate still darker moods lurking below.

'It's so—so unbelievable,' she said. That at least was safe. No one would deny that two deaths took some understanding.

'You just can't believe it,' Marius was saying to Dame Clarissa. Alicia was bringing in a tea tray. 'Why would anybody want to kill two of the greatest living pianists? Well—they *were* living. Both Italian, both mature, both very expensive commodities. But quite different in every other way. I don't believe they even knew each other.'

Dame Clarissa accepted a cup of tea and a biscuit from Alicia. 'Thank you, my dear!' She sipped politely. 'Were they known to anyone here? Personally known, I mean.'

'Not as far as I'm aware. Jim collects Alessandri records, I believe, but that's not unusual. Craig saw him at a concert in America, ages ago. I met him in Europe two years ago to sign contracts. Not quite the substance of which murder is made.'

'Beverly—who does generate the most awful ideas, as we know—suggested Mr Princeton.' Dame Clarissa looked for Marius's reaction. He smiled palely.

'Hal is just bearable as a critic. Sad as a man. A bit of a walking tragedy, I always think.' He made the gesture of drinking. 'But I can't see him shooting anyone, can you?'

'Could he be roused musically for any reason?'

'Surely not in that way,' Alicia said. 'He always seems to be to be very gentle—almost effeminately so. And I know he enjoyed both performances.'

'Mave Cardwell would be a better nomination,' Marius suggested. 'She has all the strength that Hal hasn't. But music isn't her bag at all. She comes to some of the concerts, but her heart's on the dramatic stage.'

They drank together, each following a line of thought.

'*Must* it be someone within the festival?' Alicia asked. 'There's over a million people out there. Couldn't it be someone we don't even know?'

'Someone who hates pianists? Someone who hates *Italian* pianists?' He paused, his face revealing pain. 'Someone who knew where Alessandri would be at lunch-time today?'

Silence descended like a cold fog. 'Couldn't it be that girl?' Alicia said at last, hopefully.

Marius smiled at her. 'She wasn't here for Ligorno.'

'Well, couldn't she have done in Alessandri? Must it be one?'

'Could we really cope with two?' They regarded each other with the uncomplicated gaze of people who know each other very well. Dame Clarissa glanced from one to the other.

'My dears, you mustn't let this hurt you too much.'

Marius put out a hand to her and she held it, warm, lively flesh against her own withered dryness.

'More tea, Clarissa?' Alicia said, wanting to cry.

Jim Fletcher sat on the edge of his chair, facing Verdun. He felt as if he had been summoned to see the headmaster. Verdun was putting a sheaf of papers in order, giving Jim time to relax. When he looked up, he saw that he might just as well not have bothered. The man was tense to a ridiculous level.

'Now, Mr Fletcher!'

'I don't see what I can tell you.'

'Just answer my questions. Where were you at lunch-time today?'

Jim moistened his lips. 'Well—most of the time I was in my office. There was a press release to get out. I was there until—well, I suppose about mid-day. But I don't remember looking at my watch.'

'Did you go anywhere during that time?'

His face creased anxiously. 'Go anywhere? No—well, to the toilet, I think. Not out of the building. Not until about—oh, twelve-thirty, I'd say.' He stopped. 'When was...when did...?'

'About twelve-thirty, we believe.'

'Oh!' Jim sat up, shocked. 'Well, I don't think I've got a—a whatsit?—an alibi. No one came into my room while I was working. I went out through the side door, so no one saw me then, and I sat down by the river with my lunch box until about one.'

'Did anyone see you come back?'

'I don't know. Does it matter?' He gazed anxiously at the detective.

'Not at this moment, I suppose.' Verdun kept a slightly threatening note in his voice. 'Are you married, Mr Fletcher?'

'No, I'm engaged.'

'Wedding arranged?'

'Not exactly. A couple of months, probably. Why?'

Verdun shook his head and made a note in his book. 'Not important.'

Jim stared, clearly upset. 'You don't need to know about Mary.'

'No. But I need to know about you.' Verdun put the routine questions to him, then said, 'Did you ever meet Signor Alessandri? Before? Did you know him?'

'Not personally. How would I? I don't move in those circles.'

'What did you think of him?'

Jim considered. 'Better at a distance. Close to, he lost a bit of his charm. But a fabulous musician. No one could take that from him.' He caught Verdun's eye. 'A great loss.'

'Can you see any reason why he and Mme Ligorno should have been murdered? However slight?'

'No.' Jim shook his head slowly. 'It seems—well, incomprehensible. Both of them! Makes it even odder.' Verdun indicated that the interview was over, and Jim stood. 'I'm sorry I can't be more help.'

'Everything helps,' Verdun said gravely, and Fletcher glanced at him, disturbed.

'Well—good! Yes...' He left the room, his mind turning over what he had said, what construction the detective might put on it. He wished he could think of a watertight alibi.

Verdun looked down at his notes. Alibis, it seemed, were in short supply. He gave a deep sigh. It had been a hell of a day so far. He picked up his phone and offloaded a few routine matters on to Briggs.

15

The body had been discreetly stowed away, the recital room tidied up. Marius stood by the raised dais, wanting to pay his respects to a man who, whatever had been his human failings, had been a very great performer.

As he left the hall, he wished he had stayed home. Someone had seen him enter; there were reporters and photographers lying in wait all over the town, it seemed, ready for any crumb they could catch. 'Sorry!' he said, brushing past. 'No comment at this point.'

The festival's final flourish was now in sight—a grand performance of the Bach B minor Mass with combined local choirs and the symphony orchestra in full, magnificent cry. But before that there was the last of the chamber music groups, the American Brammar Trio, and their plane was due in the small hours. Much as he wished to shed the responsibility, he knew he must meet them himself, and be ready, in particular, for any rumpus there might be at the airport over the recent tragedies.

Alicia insisted that she would accompany him. The Brammar three were known to them from past festivals, and if it hadn't been for the pall suspended over all of them he would have been looking forward to the reunion. Now...?

Well, Verdun had taken the step of providing a protective guard to escort them from airport to hotel, and a man would be on duty outside each bedroom for as long as Montagu Brammar and his companions were in the city.

If it was hardly the normal way to enjoy meeting old friends; still there was a sense of expectancy, which in part restored Marius's sagging enthusiasm. Perhaps their luck would change? Perhaps a completely unknown person would be found, confessing to both crimes? Perhaps, somehow, they would find their way back to how it was before? But he knew that he was asking too much.

Nevertheless, as he stood with Alicia, waiting for those doors to open through which Alessandri had so recently passed, Marius's spirits rose a little, quite unreasonably. He knew Montagu Brammar well, an ebullient, rotund little man with sausage-like fingers which seemed totally unsuitable for mastering piano keys. His trio members, Charles Pegler and Alan Corelli, were lanky, laconic Americans, elegant in evening dress, wizards at their skills; Charles with a violin in his hands created a magic that was challenged in every note by Corelli's marvellous way with a cello. Together the three men spun enchantment.

Marius could see plain-clothes policemen hovering in the background. He knew they would follow his hired limousine back to the hotel through the lemon dawn. He knew, too, that he himself would not rest easy until he had seen the visitors on to the plane at the end of their stay. If someone had handed him a telegram to say that the trio had been permanently delayed...well, that wasn't going to happen.

'There they are!' Alicia said suddenly, and moved swiftly to the arrival door. Brammar, reaching barely to her chin, flung his arms wide and embraced her, turning then to grasp Marius's hand with muscular fingers. All at once they were laughing and chattering together, the Hogbeins released from gathering tension into a 'high' that swept them out of the building into the limousine almost without thinking.

'And are we at risk?' Brammar asked, mischievously, as they drove into the city, the dawn glowing apricot behind them.

Marius's mood took a dive. He shook his head slowly.

'My dear Monty,' he said carefully, 'how can anyone tell any longer what is safe—or *who* is safe? You can imagine how we have been feeling. There are police following us now—and they'll be close to you throughout your entire stay.'

The trio exchanged glances, but Alicia, watching them, saw no indication of withdrawal.

'A flute-playing friend of mine in Los Angeles was killed by an automobile,' Alan said, shrugging. 'It's a dangerous world.'

Monty Brammar chuckled. 'We avoid offending our audiences.'

'If only it were that easy,' Marius sighed. Monty's fat face suddenly fell into solemn lines.

'Forgive me! It is not a joking matter for you, old buddy. Are the police making progress?'

'Not that anyone can see. Motiveless crimes, my friends. How can you pin it down when there seems to be no reason?'

They arrived at the hotel, subdued and weary. On the wide steps Alan Corelli suddenly stopped, pointing to the eastern sky, where a golden rim lit the clouds on the horizon and pale saffron was spreading up into the ice blue of the dawn sky above them.

'And yet the sun still rises!' he said softly. 'We should not take ourselves too seriously.' They stood for a moment in silence as the morning miracle unfolded, a command performance, it seemed, for them alone.

Then, behind them, the guardian police moved closer and the spell was broken. As they entered the foyer, Alicia took Marius's hand, and he held on very tightly.

'We shall certainly sleep,' Monty said. 'It's been a long journey. So we shall see you perhaps at dinner?'

Marius nodded. They watched as the three men, with baggage, instrument cases and police, disappeared into the lift.

'Pray God,' said Marius is a low voice, 'that the cops will prove to be wasting their time.'

Mave scrounged another complimentary and took Hal to the theatre to cheer him up. He was deeply depressed by a concept of 'ultimate and inevitable destruction', which he had linked in his mind with the deaths of Ligorno and Alessandri.

The play was 'The Crucible', a favourite of Mave's, but they hadn't got far into it before she realised that as a 'cheerer-upper' it was hardly a success. Hal sank in his seat, mesmerised by the awfulness of everything. So she took him out for a late supper at the Night Owl, a restaurant often used by theatre crowds and concert-goers.

It was hard work reviving him, though he seemed slightly improved after a glass of wine. Mave ordered spaghetti bolognese, and Hal settled for a ham omelette and chips. They ate in silence for a while, each lost in personal lines of thought.

'They're so disciplined,' Mave said suddenly. 'Such wonderfully controlled acting. Didn't you think so?'

Hal chased a chip around his plate. 'What discipline?'

'The way they move. The team-work—the voice control—wonderful.'

'So they should be. Top company. World reputation.'

'Doesn't always work.' Mave wound a piece of spaghetti round her fork. 'But it sure did tonight.'

'Discipline!' Hal said with a trace of bitterness. 'You think *that* was discipline? Compared with musicians, actors don't know the meaning of the word!'

Mave stared at him, then gave a surprised laugh. 'What's eating you? Of course they were disciplined. Their whole presentation, their timing...'

'Timing? Compared with orchestral musicians...' He waved his fork at her. '*That's* timing! Split second timing. Precision movement. A tenth of a second—a hundredth of a second—too late! You can't match that on a theatre stage.'

'That's not discipline!' Mave was outraged. 'That's regimentation. At least actors are free to express themselves in their roles!'

'Self-expression? Oh, dear! Was that what it was? Self-expression?' He pushed his plate away, poured and drank another glass of wine.

Mave glared at him. 'I took you to the theatre. I've brought you out for supper. What's the matter with you, Hal? You're behaving like a creep.'

'You cannot buy my opinions, you know. I know what I'm talking about. Music is the most disciplined of the arts. Look at painting—daubs, these days. No *knowledge* behind it. Look at the dramatic arts!' There was scorn in his voice—scorn and alcohol.

'Look at ballet!' Mave said, leaning forward and pushing a finger at his shirt. 'Ha! You see!'

'Ballet,' he said loftily, 'is music. First and foremost.'

'I'm sure Nureyev would agree,' she retorted acidly. 'You're a fool, Hal Princeton.' She turned away, offended. 'Oh, my God!' Sir Beverly Stainer was approaching.

'Ha, there, you two!' Sir Beverly bellowed. 'There you are! Don't mind if I join you.' It was in no way a question.

'As a matter of fact, yes,' Hal said, but too low to get through the knight's protective system. Mave took a deep breath.

'We are having a business meeting, Sir Beverly.'

He drew a chair from a neighbouring table and sat heavily, squatly, puffing tobacco-laden air as he nodded at each of them in turn.

'Been to see the acrobats. Bloody good! Bloody funny!'

'Bloody hell!' Hal muttered.

'We've been to "The Crucible",' Mave said clearly, making the best of an impossible job.

'What's that—a night club?' Sir Beverly waved imperiously at a waiter. 'What's on the menu? What've you been eating?' He peered at their abandoned plates. 'Looks revolting' The waiter arrived. 'A steak— big steak! With mushrooms and all the trimmings. Rare! Rare, mind you.' He turned to Mave. 'Like to see the juices run.'

She leaned away from him slightly. 'Yes—I bet you do.'

'And wine! Bring the wine list,' he shouted after the waiter.

'How can you eat all that at this time of night?' Mave said, fascinated. She had to say it twice before it got home, and the second time it attracted attention from several nearby tables. Even Mave was somewhat abashed.

'Always been a big eater. Remember when the wife was alive—always had a big late supper.'

'But didn't it keep you awake?'

'Nothing keeps me awake. Once I'm tucked up—the wife used to comment on it. "Bev," she used to say, "you'll miss the last trump!" No, I always slept well.'

'I never knew your wife,' Mave said, trying to alter the direction of the conversation.

'Good woman,' he said, tearing open a bread roll and plastering it with butter. 'Kept me on the straight and narrow! A man needs a good woman. The wife was all of that. Though she knew her place. "You make the decisions, Bev," she used to say, "and I'll abide by them".'

'You were a lucky man,' Mave said, wondering how long before the Lib movement Lady Stainer had passed on.

'I was a lucky man,' he said, leaning back and revealing a great deal of shirted stomach in the process. It was clear he hadn't heard her. 'Yes, the wife was one in a million!' (Hal turned his head away, but Mave had heard his muttered, 'Must have been!')

'You know,' the old man said, well into the subject, 'I had only to say to the wife, "How about flying to Sydney for the weekend?" and it was as good as done. Wonderful organiser, the wife. Made mincemeat of any secretary I've ever had. Clear vision, you see.' He leaned towards Mave. 'Could analyse a situation as soon as look at it.' He leaned back and adjusted his napkin, glancing around him for the waiter.

Silence fell. Mave was just about to signal to Hal that it was time to leave when Sir Beverly, who had apparently been deep in thought, suddenly turned to her.

'You married?'

Mave jumped. 'No—no, I'm not.'

'Ever been?'

'Yes.' She saw no reason to elaborate.

'What happened?'

She drew back, then relaxed, shrugging. What the hell! She needn't reveal her last, disastrous bend at matrimony. 'I was widowed.'

'Long time?'

'Yes. I was in my twenties.'

'Sick, was he?'

Mave regarded him thoughtfully. *Well*, she thought, *if you wanna know you gotta ask, I suppose!* 'No. He was a rigger. Killed in an explosion. Forty years ago now.' Sir Beverly nodded slowly, and if he was absorbing the information through a kind of mental osmosis. The knowledge stored, he turned heavily to stare at her, head lifted, eyes narrowed. 'As if I'm a horse,' she hazarded, glaring back at him. 'Or a mare! Or a filly…what do I do if he wants to examine my fetlocks? Or teeth?'

'Never thought of marrying again? Fine state, matrimony. Recommend it!'

'Once or twice.' She kept her voice cool.

'Defence against loneliness. You lonely?'

She bit her lip, suddenly so outraged that she wanted to laugh. 'No.'

He sat back. 'Ah! I am. Wouldn't think it to look at me. Plenty of money, this world's goods. Title, position, influence. But lonely—that's the bottom line.'

'I'm sorry,' she said, trying to feel sympathy. He nodded again, mandarin-like.

'I've often thought, y'know—if I could find a good woman, a strong-minded woman—a woman with a caring nature…' He drifted to a halt, and then his eyes slipped round to watch her, slyly, as if he were judging how she was receiving his confidences. Mave caught Hal's gaze on her in a quizzical expression which had quite eliminated his *weltschmerz!* Damn him, the man was laughing at her.

'Sounds wonderful, Sir Beverly,' she said, picking up her handbag. 'I hope you find her.'

'What do you think of this murder lark, then?' he said, tucking into his steak with gusto, a great bumble-bee flitting crushingly from one conversational flower to the next.

Mave subsided, trapped. 'I think it's horrible.'

With a physical effort Sir Beverly turned himself towards Hal, who had hoped to remain undiscovered. 'What do *you* think, Harvard?'

'Princeton,' Hal said without much hope. 'It's tragic.'

'Bloody tough on old Hogbein.'

'And on the murderees!' Hal fixed him with a venomous glare.

'And tough on the ones that got done in.' (Hal raised his eyes to heaven). 'Think it's over? Or will there be more?'

Mave picked up her bag with grim purposefulness. 'I don't think we should talk about it like this,' she said, firmly and clearly. 'We must be going, Sir Beverly.' Hal stood and pushed his chair in tidily. The old man looked up at them, surprised.

'Must you go? Ah, well, I suppose it's late. You need your beauty sleep.' Mave opened her mouth, then shut it tight. She could not protest at the top of her voice—and besides, it was no more than the truth. 'Well, well…' he cut another slice of blood-red flesh, 'I'll be seeing you.' Then he looked directly at Mave, waving his knife in her face. 'Don't forget what I said. About loneliness. Meant every word! Let me know.'

She was outside the restaurant before she could speak. 'Was that a proposition?' she said to Hal, and he, to her mortification, suddenly giggled.

'A proposal, I think. Lady Stainer—it suits you! Money, position, influence—what was it? "This world's goods". You'll be the envy of the critic's circle!'

Mave snapped at him crossly. She could ignore the heavy-handed proposal. But she wished the old fool hadn't mentioned loneliness.

'I'll drive you home,' she said, unusually grim. Hal, knowing her well, shut up and concentrated on his own throbbing head.

16

Nick Verdun finished off a damp sandwich and started on a crumbling sausage roll. It always seemed to him one of the minor paradoxes of his job that when he needed proper sustenance— while he had his nose firmly on the trail— he had to make do with curling, soggy lettuce leaves and indigestible pastry. He had a sudden desire for a good baked dinner with browned pumpkins and potatoes richly crisp on the outside and floury within; but he finished the sausage roll, trying not to taste it.

He could almost recite his notes now. They provided a good idea of where everyone had been, everyone who counted, when each of the murders had been perpetrated. He felt that he was getting to know the main characters in these obscure, annoying crimes. Yet, however much he *felt* he knew, he was for ever at the mercy of what people told him; and unless a criminal lacked the necessary low cunning to cover his activities, nothing could ever be taken for granted.

Constable Briggs had given him the results of fingerprints and the tests for gun residue. There had been some resistance from the festival people over these, but Briggs had managed to show some sensitivity (which had surprised Verdun), and won them round. Had they forgotten anything? He didn't think so. He had been given permission by Marius to look around the offices, in the hope that someone had forgotten something that would yield a clue, any clue. He was very short of clues in this case.

The notes came out again as he wiped mouth and fingers and flicked crumbs on to the floor. He, like the festival folk, had hoped that perhaps—just perhaps—an outsider had shot Ligorno, slinking into the hotel for some irrational reason (could reason be irrational? Verdun asked himself). But Alessandri's death had considerably narrowed the field. And when Verdun had interviewed the hotel manager he had been assured that at nightfall all the back entrances to the building were securely locked, and the front door could only be opened by the night porter.

The second death should have produced some link, some reason, some motive. Here, far from the European circuit, it should surely not be too difficult to find something to connect the delightful Mme Ligorno with the ineffably elegant Signor Alessandri? But any connection eluded him.

'One,' he muttered, going over it for the umpteenth time, 'they were both Italian. But—two, they seem not to have known each other. Three, no one seems to have known them personally—no one here. Who knew,' he chewed at the top of his pen, '*knew* that Alessandri was going to the recital room?'

That was easy enough, surely? Anyone at the festival office could have known; anyone in the King's Hall management. It seemed most unlikely that anyone else could have discovered the pianist's movements, made so much as an afterthought. So who else did he have? He looked up: Briggs had just entered. 'Go through this with me, Briggs.' He frowned at his notepad; Briggs sat down in the chair opposite and prepared to think. 'We need to keep a completely open mind. No one should be eliminated. So—let's start at the top with Marius Hogbein. I know…' He glanced up at Briggs. 'It's not likely that a man whose whole life was taken up in planning ongoing festivals would risk destroying his life's work in such a fashion.'

'But criminals do the weirdest things,' Briggs suggested. 'If they didn't, they wouldn't get caught.'

'That's what's worrying me,' Verdun admitted. 'These are intelligent people. They're not really criminals...we have to see into their minds, their way of thinking. I've met "one-off" crims before, and they are a different breed. Murder may be one of the most heinous crimes, but often the murderers are quite decent people, except for one over-riding compulsion—they see something they feel they have to put right, and it includes someone's death.'

They worked together down the list of names. It was tempting, for instance, to eliminate the women, but there was nothing about the shootings to rule them out. But—Coral Stone? Alicia Hogbein? Little Gwenny? There was the girl at the concert hall complex where the recital room was located. But she had been away from the city for the first murder. He grinned suddenly, and Briggs looked up.

'Dame Clarissa,' Verdun said. 'She's strong-minded enough, for sure. But she wouldn't need a gun. One withering look would kill!'

'What about Tabitha?' Biggs said hesitantly. 'Shouldn't we have another look at her? If we could pin both murders on her...'

'An unworthy thought, Briggs' but he was still grinning. 'She wasn't in the running for Ligorno's murder, and the gun was definitely the same for each killing. Let her go, Briggs.'

'Pity! I still think...'

'You want to interview her? You could go and put the fear of God into her.'

'No, thanks very much.' Briggs was adamant. 'She puts it into me!'

'Had a go at you, did she?'

'You might say.' He looked embarrassed. Verdun was amused.

'You did well to escape. She's an expert in her own line of work.' He suddenly sighed. 'We really need to find that gun.' He sat up straight, refusing to let the post-prandial urge to sleep overtake him. 'I can't see there's much use in searching at the festival office, and there's enough intelligence behind these murders to make it certain that searching their private dwellings would probably be useless. But we may have to do that.'

'I bet it won't be found, not with that spread of river outside. It could have been dropped off a ferry. And there's lakes in the suburbs—or there's zillions of hectares all around the city. Unless...' he gave a sudden shiver, 'unless it's waiting somewhere to do the job again.'

Verdun looked up. 'Don't! I can't even contemplate that. We have to hope that the two were...' He rubbed his head. '*Why?*' he said, almost angrily. 'What possible motive?' He picked up the phone and checked that the police guards were in place for the Brammar Trio. Because two pianists had been shot, it hardly followed that it would happen again. But since most of the international artistes had completed their performances and gone home, the three Yanks should have full protection. Just in case. He swore under his breath, and Briggs regarded him with interest. Verdun was noted among his peers for his calm approach to the problems of criminality; he was seeing another side of the man.

'I've never enjoyed looking for criminals among respectable citizens,' Verdun said suddenly. He stood up. As he did so, Marius Hogbein's head came round the sergeant's door, very hesitantly.

'They told me you were in here,' he said in a voice from which all the bounce had gone. Verdun waved him in. 'I shouldn't have come. Alicia told me I shouldn't. But I can't rest.' He sat down, rubbing his hands over his face. 'No news, I suppose?'

Verdun shook his head. He liked this man, but he must keep his personal feelings out of it. It would be even worse of he had to arrest a man he had come to think of as a friend.

'Nothing yet. You'll be the first to know when anything turns up.' He wanted to say 'if it ever does', but it would be ill-advised to show a lack of confidence. He turned to Briggs, handing him a photo. 'Take this down to the ferry terminus, Briggs. See if anyone remembers him.'

Briggs looked down at it; it was a snap of Craig Schuster. He looked up quickly.

'Go and do it,' Verdun said firmly, and the young officer left, wondering.

'I wish I had any ideas,' Marius sighed. 'But it still seems like a nightmare. Inexplicable! Inconceivable!'

'What do you know about your two young men? Before they came to you, I mean. Fletcher and Schuster. Both musicians, are they?'

'Craig is. You need someone who knows the cultural scene in that position. Jim came from an advertising agency. He wanted a change. This is a much more personalised job for him. You meet people, you're in touch.'

'They couldn't possibly have known either deceased?' Nick said with dwindling hope.

'They never mentioned it—before. But then I doubt if they would if they were—were planning anything.' Marius suddenly exploded. 'Oh, my God, how could I even be thinking such a thing?'

Verdun nodded sympathetically. 'We're checking everybody's background. I'm sure you'd expect that.'

'Everyone?'

'Everyone!' Verdun met the other's eyes calmly.

'The women too? Oh, that's ridiculous.'

'I know.' Verdun stood dismissively 'It would be a great help if the guilty party would just come forward and admit it. It's what I always hope for. But I don't often get it.' He saw Marius to the door.

'You're checking on me, too, I suppose?' Verdun nodded. Marius left without further comment, and the detective wandered back to his desk. There were two papers there, one headed Fletcher, the other Schuster. All that he had been able to discover about them lay open to his gaze. And seemed to get him nowhere. Just average young men, moving from job to job to improve themselves. Nothing suspicious. Nothing suspicious anywhere.

Montagu Brammar nodded in friendly fashion to the young policeman who had spent the night outside his bedroom. 'Still here, you see!'

'Glad to see it, sir.'

Together they took the lift to the ground floor, making desultory conversation. As the doors opened they saw Alan Corelli and Charles Pegler ahead of them. 'We shall be fine now, officer,' Brammar said hopefully, but the policeman shook his head, grinning faintly.

'You don't get rid of us so easily, Mr Brammar! We have our orders.'

Brammar shrugged and laughed. 'At least you're eating well.'

'Beats sitting outside a suspect's house at midnight in a winter gale!' They separated in the dining room, Montagu to join his friends, the constable to a table in one corner where the management, somewhat grudgingly, was accommodating Verdun's boys.

Alan Corelli poured milk on his muesli. 'I guess it'll be a relief to get away from here. I feel as if I'm on show.'

'A demonstration model,' Charles said. 'A specimen under glass!'

Monty tucked his napkin into his shirt, preparatory to attacking a full 'English' breakfast. 'I feel responsible. If the killings follow their pattern, I shall be the next to go.' He smiled merrily at the waitress who brought his bacon, sausage and eggs with tomatoes (optional).

Charles regarded him over his coffee cup. 'You're taking it very lightly.'

'Why should I worry? Apart from you two, I don't have an enemy in the world.' His egg, stabbed to the heart, bled all over the plate. Alan, an abstemious eater, shuddered gently at the sight.

'All it needs is one,' he said, sipping his Earl Grey with lemon.

'But seriously,' Monty said, surgically removing a piece of bone from a bacon rasher, 'who would want to kill *me*? Ridiculous! No motive, no sense in it.'

'Who would have wanted to kill La Ligorno? Or the oh-so-beautiful Signor Alessandri?' Charles poured another cup of coffee, loaded it with sugar. 'Several husbands, maybe, jealous of the marauding Piers, from all accounts. But why here?'

'Preventive therapy, perhaps.' Alan pushed his chair back. 'Charles, you will surely kill yourself with sugar! Monty, you are disgusting at breakfast! I shall go for a walk with my bloodhound.' He waved towards the police table and left, walking briskly so that his bodyguard, halfway through a second piece of toast, was hard put to catch up. Charles leaned back and regarded Monty with an expression quite free of mockery.

'You'll be careful, old friend, won't you?'

Monty nodded. 'I'm no fool, Chuck. I shall be glad to get away, too. But I have to be realistic. Where would the motive be?'

'What were the motives for the other two?'

Monty sighed. 'We shall give the performance of our lives tonight,' he said, unusually subdued. Then his face lit up with the irrepressible grin. 'And tomorrow we shall run like hell!'

17

Clem Zacaria stood at the barre in the ballet company's rehearsal room. He liked to do an hour or so each morning to keep his body pliable and his muscles in good trim. Though he wouldn't have admitted it for money, he was nearly forty-seven, and the frame had a sneaky way of protesting when he demanded that it should operate like a twenty-year old.

He swung his leg high, ignoring the sensation of tightness in his groin. He knew he would die if he had to accept the onset of old age—a long, hard death it would be, a battle to the final breath, no giving in, no graceful acceptance. He was a dancer, it was in his blood; and without it…

There was a poster of Helpmann on the wall, Helpmann as an old man, still on stage, mincing around to the music, but old, *old*! He, Clementi Zacaria, must never grow old like that. It must be one day working, as now, at the barre, the next struck down like a young god who had angered the old ones, a bolt of lightning, perhaps, a shooting star, something that would leave him bodily whole so that *they*, his public, could gaze on him and lament the life so cruelly snatched from him, exclaim over the beauty that remained even in death.

He regretted the western custom of closed coffins. Maybe he should return to Russia, where these things were handled differently.

Perhaps he could make a ballet out of it? He stared at himself in the spotted mirror, inspected his teeth, his tongue, his eyeballs, his chin. Thinning hair, carefully coiffured, curled and blond-tipped, capped his bony, chiselled head. It was good!

Moving backwards a little, he stood motionless, feet in second position, arms just so, belly firmly tucked in. Good—it *was* good! But then the image crumbled. The face—the face! He glared at himself. The face betrayed him. That was not the face of a young god. It was like that terrible, disgusting story he once read—about the handsome Dorian Gray, whose pact with the Devil meant that he could keep his beautiful face, sin and worry free, until death, his sins horribly accumulating on a once-lovely portrait.

'But I am the evil portrait!' Clem mourned in a hotch-potch of European tongues. 'I am mocked by ze Teufel—I am shunned by ze world—I am a man ze most tragique, ze most plein de tristesse! Gott in Himmel, was ist for me?'

Tears ran down his face and for a moment he seriously considered smashing the treacherous mirror. Then he remembered the sheaf of unpaid bills on his desk, and smashed his hands together instead. A very small, very new ballerina, entering cautiously to find a mislaid shoe, regarded him with large, frightened eyes.

'Is no use!' Clem cried wildly in a voice full of tragic overtones, running past her with measured steps as if leaving the stage after a solo. At the door he stopped, striking a dramatic pose, and fixed the child with a flashing eye.

'La commedia—e finita!' he said in a low, agonised whisper, and disappeared.

'Oo-er!' said the little ballerina, as the door slammed behind him.

'I must talk to everyone again. I'm sure you understand,' Verdun said. Zacaria was sitting behind his desk in an office so cluttered that it was literally impossible for a visitor to find a seat, and he was maintaining an icy dignity in face of Verdun's probing. Since his recent outburst he was feeling scoured out internally, clean, pristine, born again. He wanted nothing to spoil his post-orage purity. 'With the second murder the situation has changed somewhat. I need to know...'

'I can tell you nozzing. It is of no concern to me.'

'Unfortunately, sir, it is of considerable concern to me, and to many others. It is my responsibility...'

'Zis is not for me!' Zacaria waved a careless hand.

Verdun sighed. 'Kindly listen to me, Mr Zacaria. I have the legal right to investigate the crimes, and you are legally required to answer my questions.' He stared down on the ballet director. 'Now...'

It was hard work, and to little avail. No, Zacaria knew nothing about the Signor Alessandri. No, he was not in the vicinity of the King's Hall recital room at the time in question. He would not meet Verdun's eyes. The detective stopped for a moment, his instinct aroused. 'Are you quite sure, sir?'

'At what time?' asked Zacaria unwillingly.

'Between twelve and one.'

'Twelve and one?'

'Twelve and one!' Verdun watched him. Zacaria shrugged.

'How can I tell? I do not all ze time take out my watch and...' he snapped his fingers dramatically.

'Sir?' Verdun used his most telling professional expression, and Zacaria slowly wilted. He spread his arms wide.

'I am visiting a friend. Un ami! You comprenez? A friend who wish to be anonyme, n'est-ce pas? You are understanding?'

Verdun nodded slowly. 'A—a gentleman friend?'

'Yes, you are right, 'e is a gentleman. 'oo is working at King's 'all.' He sat up very straight and glared at Verdun. 'I do not give you 'is name. *Torture* will not tear it from me!'

'Oh, come, sir,' the detective said wearily. 'Torture is not allowed—not without a signed affidavit from three MPs and a

Roman cardinal…only joking!' he added hastily, seeing a flicker of fear in the other man's face.

'Is not joke,' Zacaria said angrily, standing and leaning over his desk, as tense and bristling as a young rooster. Verdun's control snapped without warning, and he pushed his face close to the irate Clem.

'Then kindly answer my questions!' He took a deep breath and pulled himself together. 'Please!'

Zacaria sat down slowly. 'I was in office at King's 'all at midday,' he said, subdued and pale. 'I was doing no wrong. I was not knowing he—Alessandri, is in recital room. I am leaving at twelve-fifteen—zat is all No one is seeing me after I leave.'

'Where did you go?'

Zacaria gave his expressive shrug. ''oo can tell? I am *distrait*—full of sadness.'

'Lovers' tiff?'

'Teef? What is 'teef'?

'Never mind. If you can confirm where you were, please let me know.'

Zacaria nodded. His usual eccentricity had left him; he stared up at the detective, misery in his eyes, the real kernel of a man left behind when the brittle shell was shattered. 'I am not bad man,' he said with some pathos. 'I am foolish, sometimes a little crazy—but I am not bad man, officer. I do not *kill*!'

Marius was jumpy. Alicia had given up trying to talk to him; he was alternately snappy and maudlin. They had arranged to meet Sir Beverly and Dame Clarissa in the foyer of King's Hall, and she hoped that would calm him down—though, of course, Sir Beverly was not notorious for being a calming influence.

She knew what was wrong. He was scared to death of the evening's performance, the Brammar Trio's one festival appearance. And how could she blame him? She herself felt a tingle of apprehension that made it difficult to face sitting for two hours, enjoyable though she knew it would be.

As they entered the foyer by the office door Alicia took his arm for a moment, and he gave her a wan smile.

'Courage, mon brave!' she murmured, and he paused briefly and pulled back his shoulders.

'Marchons!' he retorted, taking her hand. 'On our way! And Gawd 'elp us if...'

'Not now,' she said firmly. 'Positive thinking! Let's find the dynamic duo.'

It wasn't difficult. Sir Beverly was holding forth in stentorian tones with a mesmerised audience of four elderly city councillors; Dame Clarissa was just emerging from the 'ladies'.

'My dears!' she declaimed, advancing with arms outstretched, scarves and drifting panels floating behind her, huge pearls clanking against a large brooch in the shape of an elephant. Alicia swallowed hard as an alternative to nervous laughter. Clarissa kissed her cheek, asking 'How is dear Marius?' in a stage whisper which, had it not been for Sir Beverly's trumpeting, would have been heard across the foyer.

'He's well, thank you, Clarissa. Though worried, of course. We'll *all* be glad when this festival's over—more glad than usual.' She laughed, half-humorously. 'We're going away for a few days.'

'Very wise. *Very* wise! It's been a strain. Oh, dear...' She caught sight of Sir Beverly, his hands upheld, fingers swooping. 'I must stop him, my dear. He's started on his war stories...'

Alicia watched her gaff the old man and bring him neatly to shore. 'Good evening, Sir Beverly.'

'Good evening, Alicia. Evening Hogbein.' He swung back on his heels. 'Just bin tellin' them about that time I saw the Nasties comin' over the hill and...'

'Do shut up, Beverly! No one wants to hear about the war tonight.'

The old, man turned to Alicia. 'But I don't suppose anyone wants to hear about the war tonight. Looking forward to the show?'

'Very much.

The bell rang, and Alicia gave a sigh of sheer thankfulness. 'Come on, let's go in.'

18

Montagu Brammar bounced on to the platform followed by Charles Pegler and Alan Corelli. The two tall Americans were as smoothly elegant as herons; Brammar like a rotund little penguin. As they stood in line, bowing, Marius quite unconsciously relaxed and gave himself over to the pleasures of the music. Alicia, feeling his muscles slacken, let herself slide down a fraction in her seat. Beside her, Dame Clarissa was shushing Sir Beverly into acquiescent silence.

Marius was glad that it was Mozart first. The mathematical certainties of the period combined with the master's inspirational powers of turning those certainties to his own superb ends had a particularly soothing effect.

They were playing well, very well. Montagu's touch on the Steinway was, as ever, pure delight: the runs flowing like raindrops, crystal-clear; the lyricism never sugary, always dulcet; the moments of power defined, controlled, dynamic.

Charles and Alan played as one man, leaning towards each other, totally absorbed. Marius had forgotten just how good these three were together. His black mood left him. The cool astringencies of a specially commissioned work by young America composer Gabriel Muskett were like a wild Arctic snowscape after classical Mozartian elegance. Marius's newly cheerful mood underwent an adrenalin surge; by the interval he was ready for anything. Though perhaps not for Sir Beverly.

'Load o' bloody rubbish!' the stout knight was saying as Marius and Alicia, somewhat delayed, arrived at the VIP interval reception. 'Damn feller oughta be shot!' He saw Marius and bore down on him, one thick finger poking him in the dinner jacket. 'Oughta be shot, that's what I say!'

'*Who* should be shot?' Marius demanded, outraged; and Dame Clarissa, seeing his face, moved into action.

'Come here, you silly man.' She took Sir Beverly by the arm and led him away.

'What's the matter, eh? What's the matter?'

'I think you do it on purpose, Beverly. I really do! How *can* you, how can even *you* talk about shooting at a time like this?' Her voice carried regally across the room.

'Figure o' speech, old girl,' he said, and for once had the grace to look abashed. 'Suitable thing to do to these modern fellers. String 'em up! Do 'em in! Let them do their damned caterwauling in someone else's backyard.'

'Beverly, I'm ashamed of you.' Dame Clarissa turned her back on him and faced Marius. 'Dear boy, I know he's sickening, but have mercy on him. He's old and silly, but he means well.'

'God help us,' Marius muttered, infuriated, 'if he ever means ill!' Aloud he said, 'Think nothing of it, Clarissa. We all know Beverly.'

Conversation, which had died while the ruckus was on, filled the gaps; champagne helped. By the time the three players were well into Dvorak's Dumky Trio Marius was in control of himself again.

At the back of the stalls, Nick Verdun stood in shadows and let his eyes wander. On each level there was a policeman, and backstage a couple more. No one had suggested that there was still danger, but who could tell? If pianists were being turned into an endangered species, this was the place to be.

The end of the Dvorak was signalled by a tremendous burst of applause. Verdun thought, not for the first time, what a strange ritual it was. Cheering he could understand (and there was some of that, too), an instinctive welling up from within the heart of the listener, exploding through the vocal cords, expressing a deep-felt emotion. But this business of banging hand against hand—where had it come from? Who started it? Was it another instinct, coming from the moment when, moved by emotions, one clasped one's hands together? It was daft, if you really began to think about it. But he had to admit that fifteen hundred people all applauding together made a sound worth hearing.

So, it seemed, thought the performers. Beaming, bowing, they returned again and again; played a light, frothy exhibitionist piece as an encore, then another, slow, gentle, mesmeric, to round the whole thing off nicely. It wasn't Nick Verdun's kind of music, any of it, and he had been surprised to see yet another full house for what had always seemed to him an esoteric entertainment; but he could recognise skill and artistry when he saw them.

He slipped through the door as the waves of approbation faded away by some mutual consent, and made his way backstage. If the previous murders were anything to go by, the next few hours were the danger time.

The amount of noise coming from the downstairs lounge at the hotel indicated a large and convivial gathering; and it was indeed crammed with people, all talking nineteen to the dozen, all feeling some remnant of the magic the evening had generated—and some sensitive to the underlying mood of apprehension.

The police were there, lounge-suited, wandering quietly among the guests at this spur-of-the-moment party organised by Marius. He had not wanted to go straight home, and he suspected that others might feel the same way. Monty, when approached, had revealed fleetingly a kind of relief—that he was not doomed to be on his own? Perhaps. The pianist had kept to himself the fact that he was arranging his own safety precautions—he would spend the rest of the night on the couch in Charles's bedroom, not even letting the police in on the plan.

He would enjoy the party, go upstairs only when Charles did, and stay behind locked doors until the car came to take them to the airport. Not even Nick Verdun was to know. Alan Corelli was to distract their personal bodyguards, somehow, for a brief moment, and in that fraction of time Monty would scurry into Charles's room, the next one along the corridor from his own.

So now he was free to relax and be his normal exuberant self. He chatted, laughed, ate and drank; the low-profile police were almost forgotten.

Slowly, the party began to dissolve and break up. Marius was talking to a man with odd views about Russian music, linking it with obscure references in the Revelation of St John. He nodded and smiled and detached his mind, seeing Alicia across the room, smiling with devastating charm into the face of an elderly cleric. Sir Beverly and Dame Clarissa were at a table near the door, Mave and Hal were apparently engaged in a deep and bitter argument conducted in low voices with smiles attempting to mask the angry eyes. And members of the festival staff were scattered throughout the lounge, making themselves pleasant to admirers of the festivities, explaining policy or setbacks to the more critical.

It was not his job to watch everyone, Marius told himself firmly. Let Verdun handle that.

'I must visit the boy's room,' Monty said to Alan, putting down his glass.

'Want me to come with you?'

Monty hesitated for a moment, then grinned broadly. 'No, I'll let my guardian angel case the joint first.' He made his way towards the policeman and explained the situation to him. The young man nodded, and without drawing attention to himself went out into the foyer towards the door leading into the men's toilets.

'I shall be perfectly safe,' Monty said to Charles, who had materialised at his elbow. 'This is really rather ridiculous, don't you think?'

'But perhaps necessary.' Alan was glancing around the room, brow furrowed.

'Look!' Monty pointed. 'The door is in full view from here. Let's not get paranoid about this. When he tells me that it's all clear, I shall go. Then,' the mischievous smile returned, 'if I'm not back in two hours you can call the Mounties!'

The young policeman reappeared at the door of the men's room and nodded. Montagu slipped, almost unobserved, across the wide passageway and into the toilets, leaving the policeman outside, apparently reading a poster on the wall. Charles and Alan, drinks untouched in their hands, waited, their eyes never leaving the doorway.

He had had his eyes on Brammar, waiting for an opportunity. When he saw the pianist's gestures towards the toilets he took the chance, slipping silently away from the crowd.

If the man had not needed the toilet, there would have been other chances. He had slipped round the corner, opened the insignificant door to the cleaners' cupboard when the young cop had gone in by the other entrance. If he had been discovered they would have found the gun on him, and that would have been that. But the man didn't look in the cupboard, simply checked on all the cubicles and then reported it all clear.

When Montagu entered it was just a matter of waiting until the cubicle door closed and then slipping out quietly.

It seemed such a pity, this time. But the plan must be properly carried out. It was too late to start to make changes. He wrapped a cleaner's overall around him, put on gloves and gave Brammar time to finish, knowing that no one would be let in. When the pianist emerged, humming a melody from the Dvorak trio, he stood in front of him, the gun pointing at the little man's heart. Brammar's eyes flew wide in astonishment, and the humming stopped.

'I'm sorry about this, Mr Brammar,' he said with complete sincerity. 'I'm afraid it's unavoidable.'

The silenced shot could not possibly be heard outside the toilets, with the outer door closed and the party still noisy. Brammar stood for a moment, then his legs crumpled beneath him and he fell backwards into the cubicle, the only sound a long, perhaps surprised sigh. He lay on the cold marble floor for several seconds, looking up through gathering mists at his murderer, trying to ask 'why?'. But mist became fog, and his eyes closed in great weariness; there was no pain, he noted in his last conscious thought. That seemed odd.

The murderer stood for a brief moment, as if in silent respect for his victim. Then he stripped off the overall, threw it with the gloves into the cupboard and hurried away, out through a door the policeman hadn't thought to check, because at first sight it seemed no more than a long mirror on the wall. But it led to a storeroom and thence out into a parallel staff corridor, empty at this late hour. He would re-join the party when chaos erupted. Someone would sound the alarm before long, and no one would be counting heads for a couple of minutes, at least.

'I'm going in,' Charles said. 'He's been long enough.' Alan followed him. The way was barred by the young policeman. 'We think you should check,' Charles said quietly.

Verdun, seeing them, came across. 'Something wrong?'

'We think Monty's been in there long enough. Someone should look.'

Verdun turned to the policeman. 'I checked it out, Sergeant. No one in there. And no one's gone in since.'

'All the same,' Charles said, and Nick nodded suddenly. His heart did a double thump in his chest.

He opened the door and went in. All was quiet, but there was a lingering odour on the air that he recognised at once. Someone had fired a gun. He ran round the corner where the washbasins were to the row of cubicles, and stopped when he saw Montagu Brammar's neatly shod feet protruding from an open door. He didn't really need to see the pianist lying on the grey marble to know what he would find; the spreading stain on the once white evening short was only confirmation. Nick Verdun, his face blanched with weariness and a kind of futile anger, turned on the young copper.

'Stand by the door! Don't let anyone in or out!' The boy was looking green, as well he might. Verdun went swiftly through the men's room, opening the cleaning cupboard, noting that there would have been adequate room to hide in, finding the overall and gloves. Then he pushed the mirror door and realised that it opened into a darkened storeroom. He ran through it to open the further door and put his head out into the passageway, but there was, of course, no one there. He had not expected there would be.

Frustrated, he went back to the door where Charles and Alan were waiting, their faces pale with anxiety.

'Go and stand over that body!' he hissed in a fierce whisper to the constable. 'And don't let *anyone* come near it!'

'Something's happened, hasn't it?' Charles said, and Verdun nodded.

'Don't go in, please, Mr Pegler.' He gestured to Briggs—a silent and shocked Briggs. 'Surround this place. Ring for reinforcements. Don't let anyone enter or leave the hotel until I tell you. Get the manager for me. And move everyone into the lounge and shut the doors and guard them! The team'll be here shortly.'

Marius was staring at him over the heads of the crowd, and pulled away from the couple he was with to move quickly to Verdun's side. Verdun, answering the question in Hogbein's eyes, nodded. 'I'm afraid so.'

It seemed very likely that Marius would collapse; but after a few moments he pulled himself together. 'Shot?' he asked.

Verdun nodded again. 'I'm sorry. I'm really sorry. He was your friend.'

'But how…?'

'God knows! There's a lot to be done. No one can leave just yet.' He glanced around him. 'Will you locate all your staff and get them in one corner? I need to know where everyone is.'

There was a sudden hush in the lounge as the knowledge came to them. Marius grabbed Alicia. 'They got Monty! Help me round everybody up.' She took in the bitter anguish in his face and put out a hand to him. 'Just get everyone,' he said, pulling away. 'Over here.'

He found Coral, standing with a handkerchief to her mouth, her eyes wide with shock. Charles and Alan, distraught, were standing together as if they could warn off danger as long as they remained close. In a sudden rush, an instinctive thing, several members of the party spilled out into the corridor and confronted the police, milling around aimlessly, getting in the way.

'Get back!' Marius shouted above the hubbub. 'For God's sake get back, damn you!' Craig Schuster was at the far side of the crowd, and he too began to shepherd them back into the small lounge. 'Where's Jim?' Marius yelled. 'For heaven's sake, where's Jim?' Craig shook his head, his hand spread wide. Marius felt sick.

Verdun raised his voice commandingly. 'I shall require names and addresses of everyone who has been here for the past hour. I shall also need everyone's movements in the past fifteen minutes. When that has been done I can let you go. So it is in everyone's interest to help us take details. One at a time, please, to my men at the door.'

A horrid quiet fell on the lounge, broken only by Sir Beverly. 'We came in over the top, rifles at the ready, and saw the bastards hiding behind a tree. Picked 'em off one at a time!'

Alicia, who had more than enough, bellowed in his ear furiously. 'Shut *up*, Sir Beverly, shut *up*! A man is dead!'

For once, something registered. Sir Beverly turned slowly in his chair, seeing shocked, accusing faces on all sides. He caught Dame Clarissa's beaky gaze and his face sagged. He seemed, she thought, like a small child chastised by unreasonable adults when he had expected praise. She looked reproachfully at him.

'They were pleased at the time,' he said plaintively. 'Gave me a gong for it.'

'I know,' Clarissa said, hurt for him. 'But it's over now, Beverly. It doesn't *matter* anymore.'

Outside the glass doors Jim Fletcher stood for a moment, peering in at the subdued crowd. Marius opened the door and dragged him in.

'*Where have you been?* Where have you been, Jim?'

'I was on the phone. On the phone, Marius. Why? Has something happened?'

Hal Princeton sat with his head in his hands, smoke wreathing from his cigar; beside him, her face drawn under the black hair, Mave watched the slowly dwindling crush. Names, addresses and recent locations given to the police, the erstwhile party-goers went out silently into the night, past uniformed constables on duty, through the outer doors unlocked for them by an angry, anxious manager.

Mave was trying to remember where everyone had been during those last few minutes before the body had been found. She had a good visual memory—the fruits, perhaps, of many years of theatre-going—and she could place many in their groups, though not all. There was no doubt where the knight and the dame had been: the old man's voice had drummed in her ears, wordless reverberation cutting through the excited conversation around him. Anyway, no one could seriously think…

The same was true for Marius and Alicia, visible at all times—and to Hal, she suddenly realised. Hal, at least, could not be implicated in this latest insanity. She felt a momentary sensation of relief, and then wondered why. Had she ever seriously thought he *could* be involved? Surely not! Perhaps she had been viewing it through the eyes of the police, quite unintentionally.

'You're out of it, anyway,' she said, leaning towards him; and Hal, very slowly, lifted his head and turned painfully to regard her with red-rimmed eyes.

'Out of it? Was I ever in it? Is that what you thought?'

'Of course not, you idiot! But now *they*—everybody knows it. Face it, Hal, you'll have been on the list.'

He stared across the room blankly, then nodded sombrely. 'I suppose you're right.' He sighed deeply. 'How should one review a recital that ends in death? Tell me, O Wise One! Lend me your experience. For it seems as if every concert I attend prelude to a wake.' He stubbed out his cigar petulantly. 'Who will be next? Shall we begin on conductors? Or world-famous divas? Shall we decimate the musical profession? For what reason, you may ask? Is it an Arts Council plot to save money on grants?'

He finished off his glass of wine, placing the stem with pernickety precision on the centre of a coaster printed with the festival logo. 'Perhaps it is a ploy to make room for new blood? These—victims were all well into maturity. Perhaps we should be looking for a disgruntled young performer, or an agent with ideas for a world-shattering coup. It may be that this fair city is only the first venue in a globe-encircling conspiracy by a mad scientist to make more funds available for research...'

'What *are* you going on about, Hal?'

'Less for music, more for science! I doubt if our devoted and quite charming flat-footed friend has the qualities necessary to break a case based on the insane delusions of a mad scientist.' He closed his eyes wearily.

'I wonder,' Mave said, almost to herself, 'I wonder if it *is* madness. If so, it will be very difficult to pin down.'

'If it's madness, look no further,' Hal muttered, opening his eyes as a disturbance broke out at the doors. Clem Zacaria, wearing a strangely sinister hat something between an akubra and an artist's wide-brimmed felt, was expressing some annoyance at being kept waiting. Mave, detached, sleepy with wine and smoke and noise, and the shock of facing yet another killing, watched his posturings; and suddenly it came to her that at no time, before the murder, had she seen Clem in the lounge.

'I'd have known. I couldn't be in the same room with Clem and not know.'

Hal, eyes heavy, let his chin sink on his chest and did not ask her what she meant.

19

The body had been discreetly removed through the store room, and the last names and addresses had been taken, leaving only the central festival figures and the police in the lounge. The hotel manager and a waiter appeared at the door with cups of coffee on a tray, and their arrival penetrated a stony silence through which not even Sir Beverly had attempted to break.

Marius tried to produce a smile and failed. 'Thank you,' he said in a grimly controlled voice as a cup was handed to him. He caught the manager's cautious eye. 'You know I'm sorrier than I can say...'

'I don't suppose you could help it,' the manager said, leaving room for a faint sense of doubt. 'The owners won't exactly be pleased.'

Alicia was sitting next to her husband, with Dame Clarissa and the knight across the table. The old man was to a remarkable extent subdued, his face quite grey; Clarissa saw a fine tremble in his hand as he lifted the cup, and worried about him.

Hal was now asleep, his coffee untouched, his breath whiffling in and out through lips relaxed by alcohol's fumes. Mave, tired, and long past the mood for inquisitive excitement she had felt after Ligorno's death, wanted to go home with a great, unbearable yearning, and didn't much mind if she never saw any of these people again. Especially Nick Verdun, who was going through the lists of names and addresses with his offsider, and who looked amazingly alert, all things considered. She glared at him, suddenly angry that he had not been able to prevent this latest tragedy.

Feeling her eyes on him he glanced up, his own eyes going beyond her to a table in the far corner where Craig Schuster was sitting, legs outstretched, ankles crossed, a dark frown on his face, *his* eyes fixed on a framed picture of some Edwardian belle on the wall. Beside him, Jim Fletcher, pale, shoulders bowed, toying with his coffee spoon, meeting no one's eyes. And, standing beside a large ornamental fern on a Victorian whatnot, was Clem Zacaria, best profile presented to the room, one foot elegantly forward and a hand casually placed on hip.

Verdun wanted to laugh; the man was ridiculous. Unfortunately, that didn't invalidate him as a major suspect. For, mad as the ballet director was, perhaps the obscure motives for these killings could only be explained outside the realms of normality.

'Sir Beverly—Dame Clarissa!' Verdun gave a little bow to each. 'I believe you were in here throughout the—the period in question?' He looked at their worn old faces. 'You could have gone, you know,' he said gently. Dame Clarissa shook her head.

'We preferred to stay. We felt—responsible. And we couldn't leave Marius…' Her voice tailed off and she nodded reassuringly at both Hogbeins. Then she stood stiffly, something of her usual brusqueness returning. 'Come on, Beverly, time to go!'

Sir Beverly lumbered to his feet. 'Shockin' business,' he said, throwing a grimly reproachful glance at the detective. 'Should never have been allowed to happen.' But he was not the full-blooded, ranting figure of yore. The steam had subsided, the boilers were empty. For a moment Nick Verdun almost regretted the change. He turned to Marius.

'You and Mrs Hogbein are free to go as well.'

Marius's eyes went to the far table, a question in them, and Verdun shook his head. 'I must talk to them before I can let them leave.'

Marius nodded, accepting the unspoken suspicions. 'Then I would like to stay, if I may?' Verdun inclined his head in agreement. 'You go,' he said to Alicia, and after a moment's hesitation she took her bag and turned to Clarissa and Beverly.

'May I come with you?'

'Of course you may!' Clarissa pulled herself upright, but no one was deceived. The lady was distraught.

'Plenty of room in the car,' Sir Beverly said, but Clarissa shook her head firmly.

'We shall take a cab. There has been enough death for one night, Beverly.'

Verdun and Marius watched them go. 'It's hit the old folks hard,' Marius sighed. 'Now!' He took a deep breath. 'Let's get on with it.'

Craig Schuster sat down at Verdun's invitation in the place just vacated by Sir Beverly, and the detective sat opposite, his gaze cool and watchful, Briggs, notebook at the ready, to one side. Marius placed himself a little apart, not quite within Craig's eye-range, but in a position from which he could observe the young man.

'Mr Schuster! Your movements during this reception, please.'

Craig stared at the wall, thinking. 'I brought the trio members down here from the foyer after the performance. I got their first drinks, saw that people were beginning to chat to them—moved off and got a drink for myself.'

'Did you leave the lounge at all after that?'

'Yes...' He leaned back and slid his hands into his pockets. 'Yes—I went upstairs and got a barman to find me a sandwich. I hadn't had any dinner.'

'There was food down here.'

'Cocktail bits and pieces! I was hungry.'

'Why did you not have dinner?'

'Got caught up with things at the office, and suddenly realised the time. It often happens.'

'What things?'

'Well—for example, we're finishing in a couple of days with a huge performance of the B minor Mass. And at the last moment a soloist can't do it. I was trying to find a replacement.'

Verdun glanced at Marius, who nodded.

'And did you find one?'

'As a matter of fact, yes.' Craig turned to Marius. 'Haven't had time to tell you. Bryan Hendrick-Pond. He'll ring you in the morning.'

'Pond? Good work!'

'And later? After the sandwich?'

'I went out to the toilet. A while before—before…' He stopped. 'Then…'

'You came back here?'

'Oh, yes.' He gave a small, dry smile. 'I came back.'

'Where were you when the murder was discovered?'

Craig looked across the room thoughtfully. 'By then, I was somewhere just by the doors—the party had a tendency to spill out into the corridor, as you know. I would have been just over there, on the left.'

'Could you see the toilet door?'

'I suppose so. If I'd looked.'

'Did you see Montagu Brammar go across into the men's room?'

'No. No, I didn't see him go.'

'Were you talking to anyone at the time? Anyone who could corroborate your story?'

Craig shrugged. 'Someone must have seen me, I imagine. But I wasn't actually *with* anyone. Not then.' He smiled briefly, relaxed. 'Marius will tell you I'm a bit of a loner. Not a social butterfly.' He glanced at Marius, who agreed.

'Right!' Nick Verdun wrote a few more careful words, then looked up at the young man, and there was a coldly enigmatic, penetrating quality in his expression. He kept his eyes on his 'victim' until Craig shifted suddenly in his chair. 'Thank you, Mr Schuster. Don't leave town without telling me. I shall need to talk to you again. Good night.'

He drew a neat line at the bottom of the page, ignoring the other's departure. Marius, his stomach aching with stress and sudden hunger, tried to smile at his administrative officer, but could find nothing to say.

Verdun wrote a couple of words on his notebook and showed it to Briggs, who read it and glanced at his superior's face. He nodded and moved away towards the doors. He was thinking that, perhaps, things were moving at last.

At the far table, Jim Fletcher watched Craig leave. Beside him, Clem Zacaria was sitting, chin raised defiantly, fingers drumming irritatingly on the table-top. Everything about him said that he would sell himself dearly.

Jim had a hunched look about him as he sat down and waited for Verdun to open the batting. Marius was worried. He had watched the young man, in the days following the first murder, grow more and more withdrawn. He hoped this was simply the reflection of a compassionate, sensitive nature.

'You were not in the lounge during the time in question,' Verdun began. 'I would like a full run-down of your activities this evening after the recital came to an end.'

'He's suspicious,' thought Marius, tensely. Jim stared back at the detective.

'Well, I came here from the concert hall. With Coral. She could verify that for you.' He stopped, frowning nervously. 'I was here for quite a while. You must have seen me, Marius, surely?'

Marius nodded slowly. 'I can remember seeing you right at the start. You were talking to a woman in a greyish sort of dress, over by the door.'

'She was asking about the festival's financial situation. Whether we break even.' He glanced up, his expression lightening briefly. 'I didn't tell her!' Marius acknowledged the small quip with an appropriately small smile.

Verdun let his eyes slide over both of them. 'And after that?'

'I was half thinking about going home. I've been feeling really tired. But then someone said there was a phone call for me up in the main foyer. So I went up to take it.'

'Who was calling?'

'It was my fiancée. She was ringing from Bridgefield. At least...' He stopped. 'I *suppose* she was ringing from home. Unfortunately, by the time I got to the phone the call had been lost. Don't ask me why. So I rang her instead. But first the phone went on the blink, and then when it did ring the other end I got a wrong number. So I decided to give it away and come back to the party.'

'And did you?'

'I got halfway back. Then I suddenly got worried—about Mary. She's been hearing all these reports and so on—about the murders. It suddenly came to me that perhaps *she* was worrying in case I'm in danger—silly, but one can understand it.' He looked from one man to the other. 'You can, can't you?' he asked anxiously, and they agreed silently.

Verdun waited, and the waiting seemed to prey on Jim's nerves. Marius wanted to help him, to say, 'Look, keep cool. They'll be looking for nervousness.' But he knew he mustn't. If it was Jim they were looking for—well, three murders created a situation in which normal niceties went by the board.

'So?' Verdun asked patiently.

'So I went back and tried to get her again. On another phone. There's a box outside, just round the corner. But there was no answer. She must have been out. I don't think she's away, she'd have told me. I'm sure she would. But her parents must have been out, too.' He suddenly shook his head, as if it was all too much for him. 'It was late for her. *I* don't know!' Catching Verdun's eye on him, he said, 'Does that help?'

'Does your young lady often ring you at this hotel? Wouldn't she be more likely to call the festival office?'

Jim stared at him. 'I—I don't know. I didn't think of that.'

'And how did you know it was your young lady?'

'I—I assumed...They said it was a woman.'

Marius could visualise him adding these problems to the ever-growing pile of difficulties to be surmounted.

After a moment, Verdun asked, 'Did anyone see you? When you went out to the phone box?'

Jim shrugged, spreading his hands. 'I haven't the slightest idea. Someone might have seen me in the box. Receptionist, perhaps—though it was quite busy up there. But I didn't see anyone who could corro-corroborate that I was...But I *was* there!' he said, exploding in peevishness. 'Mary rang me, and I spent what seemed like ages trying to get in touch with her. Then I came back here—and...' All at once it appeared that he had just seen what all this was leading to, and he went even paler. 'Oh, God! Wasn't anyone else out of the room?'

'Can you tell us anything more? Anything at all?'

'About what?'

Verdun turned a leaf of his notes and started writing at the top of the page. Jim was mesmerised by the pen making its neat way across the clean paper. 'I'd like your fiancée's full name and address, and her telephone number.'

Jim shot forward in his chair. 'You're not going to pester her! No—I won't have it. Leave Mary alone. She knows nothing about any of this.'

'No one will pester her, Mr Fletcher. But she would probably be glad to confirm your story and help you establish your movements—don't you think?'

Jim closed his eyes and sighed, then gave the required details. Marius regarded him with compassion. There was a soft centre to this young man which would always be hurt by a tough world. Could he really have done anything so planned, so determined, as to take a gun and shoot even one person? It was difficult to believe. He had to remind himself that if murderers wore the mark of Cain on their foreheads in full view of the world, catching them would be a whole lot easier. He felt deeply depressed.

'You can go, Mr Fletcher,' Verdun said at last, fixing him with that quietly piercing look. Jim, shaken and disturbed, left quickly.

It was difficult to meet the detective's eyes, but Marius did so. 'What do you think?' he asked in a low voice. Verdun shrugged.

'He's very evasive in his manner. Even while he's telling all.'

'That's just Jim. He's a quiet, private person.'

'Like Schuster?'

Marius considered the two men. 'No, not like Craig. Craig is strength under a reserved exterior. Jim's a different kettle of fish. Mary is his salvation, I imagine. I've met her once—a supportive, gently strong woman who'll make a good wife in the old-fashioned way. Home and kids, *you* know. He thinks he's protecting her, but that's not how I see them.'

'Clever women never let on that they're the power in the home!' Verdun leaned back for a moment, weary. Then he glanced at the far table and saw Clem Zacaria, still sitting with his fingers beating a tattoo. 'I'd better get him over with.'

'Clem?' Marius began to smile, then realised that with three pointless murders in the bag it would be better not to joke about a man who was obviously, who in fact gloried in being, eccentric. What was more eccentric than gunning down three innocent geniuses?

Zacaria came to the seat of interrogation with carefully placed steps and sat gracefully on the hard chair provided. An expression of ineffable scorn was somewhat mitigated by a gleam of something very sane in his narrowed eyes. 'Officer,' he began, but got no further. Verdun was not about to let him take over the questioning.

'You were not in the lounge when the last murder was committed. Where were you?'

Clem's mouth, open to attack, closed abruptly. He pulled in his stomach, lifting himself in his chair, and at the same time flared his nostrils in a splendidly theatrical manner. 'I was elsewhere!'

'We know that. Where is "elsewhere"?'

'I was in my office. There is always work to do, vouz comprenez? Ze work of a ballet director demands ze 'ole 'eart, ze 'ole mind.' His accent perceptibly thickened.

'Yes, I'm sure it does. We appreciate that. But this is a simple question of your whereabouts at the time of the murder. Where were you, sir?'

Clem arranged his jacket around him like a dowager settling her furs. 'Are you accuse me, officer?' Verdun stared at him thoughtfully, determined he would show no impatience.

'I am asking, Mr Zacaria. *Asking!* Where were you this evening? And can anyone vouch for you?'

'I am in my office. Since many hours. No one is seeing me. That is all I am saying.' He froze in a posture of defiance. All at once, and quite unexpectedly to himself and to Verdun, Marius lost his temper.

'For God's sake, you blithering ass, *will you answer the questions?*' He stood up, leaning across the table and glaring at the astonished Zacaria. Verdun, caught unawares, turned towards him. 'Tell us where you were, who saw you, what you were doing! But talk, damn you! Talk! Stop behaving like a third-rate provincial ballerina. You're in trouble, Zacaria, we're all in trouble. *Answer the bloody questions!*'

Zacaria's mouth hung open. The police, still collating information at the other side of the lounge, stared in mild alarm. Verdun, who had considered the value of shutting him up until he saw the look on Zacaria's face, leaned back in his chair, not sorry to hand the fireworks over to someone else. Marius, suddenly aware of what he was doing, sank down and put his head in his hands.

'No one,' Clem said slowly, stunned, 'is seeing me' His eyes never left Marius's bowed head. 'But I am seen by girl at reception desk of 'otel. She is saying so kindly that she have seen me dance and enjoyed it. I was very moved. She is pretty girl.' He hurried on when he saw Verdun brow lowering in a frown. 'Ze waiter is seeing me at the top of zese stairs. I am asking him for fresh-squeezing orange juice. He is saying yes, but orange juice is not coming. I am understanding zat zere is some drama, some...' He stopped, searching for words. 'It is murder again, but I am not knowing zis until I come down ze stairs.' He glanced away from Marius to bend a beseeching gaze on the detective. 'I tell you before—Zacaria is not bad, 'e is only a little mad. 'e does not shoot peoples, could not shoot true artiste. 'e 'as soul of artiste 'imself—'ow shall 'e destroy ze gift of God?' He crossed himself quickly and subsided in his chair, a forlorn and faintly comic figure. Verdun pondered for a moment.

'Don't leave town, Mr Zacaria. You may go now, but I may wish to see you again.' The ballet director stood, all the bounce gone; he turned to leave, but then stopped and put a hand on Marius's shoulder. Marius, heavy with shame, did not look up.

'We 'ave been good friend to each ozzer, Marius. Shall we lose zis now?' Marius shook his head slowly, as if it were almost too heavy to move.

'Sorry, Clem.'

When Zacaria had left, Verdun closed his notebook and made to stand up. Marius glanced up at him. 'I do apologise. I've been under great strain, but that isn't really a good enough excuse for what just happened.'

Verdun grinned at him. 'It had the required effect. Most dramatic! I was almost ready to confess myself.'

'Thank you.' They stood together, both weary, both caught in a web of someone else's making, and let the evening's traumas go a little. As they went towards the door, Marius suddenly gave a hard, self-conscious laugh. 'It certainly got him going, didn't it? I must try it again sometime.' Then the brief mood evaporated. 'Are you any nearer knowing?' His eyes implored.

Verdun hesitated. 'Let's say it's beginning to make a pattern. I know who didn't do it, and that's always a help. The circle is narrowing. We need someone to panic, make a mistake, think he's got away with it.'

'Will there be any more?'

'Are there any more pianists?' He raised his eyebrows. 'I'm not making a macabre joke. I think it's important—that they were all pianists. I don't pretend to know why. But that can't be a coincidence, surely?'

Marius shook his head. 'No more pianists, not at the moment.'

'Then we must pray for an error of judgement on the part of the murderer.'

At the door they separated. Marius drove home slowly, the policeman's last words in his ears. Somewhere among his friends was someone who must now be known as—The Murderer! It was an ugly thought.

20

Alicia was waiting with a cup of hot chocolate. Marius was grateful for it. It was more comforting than alcohol. 'You've had enough booze for one day, anyway,' she said firmly. 'Take off your shoes and try to relax.'

For a few moments they were quiet, sitting on opposite sides of the empty fireplace, the room lights low and restful. Then Marius stirred. 'I made a bloody fool of myself.'

'That's unusual!' Alicia said with wifely sarcasm. 'What about?'

'I lost my temper with Zacaria.'

Alicia smothered a laugh. 'Has he vowed eternal enmity?'

'No, funnily enough. He was quite subdued afterwards. I think perhaps he needed something to bring him down to earth, where the rest of us live.'

'Was he being obstructionist?'

'The worst! Oh, Alicia—what on earth will come out of all this? I daren't think about it. The whole thing terrifies me.' He caught her sympathetic eye. 'You know they—Verdun thinks it has to be either Jim or Craig. Or Zacaria. Too many of us were eliminated tonight. It's a question, so Verdun says. Of hoping that *the murderer*—that's one of our friends he's talking about—the murderer will make a mistake and give himself away. I don't know what to do, Alicia. I don't know how to go on facing them, those three men. One of them must be mad, and it's too easy to say that Clem's the most likely candidate. I doubt if his madness runs in this kind of direction.'

'Then what do you think?' she said gently, seeing his distress. 'Do *you* have any idea which it might be?'

He turned sad eyes on her. 'How can I even make a guess? I've worked with these men.' He came across and knelt in front of her, and she took his head in her arms and held him quietly. After a while he moved and she released him. 'I hope to God it'll all be over soon. I don't know how much more of this I can take.'

'Bed!' Alicia said wisely. 'It's after three o'clock. You'll be fit for nothing in the morning.'

When the bedside lights went out, Marius stared upwards in the dark. 'Every day you read about murders,' he said in a voice not far from tears. 'I never realised…never thought…'

Alicia put out a hand and touched him. 'Sleep! The world's no worse than it was because it's hitting home to us. Once it's over…' But she could not go on. Marius held her hand tightly, like a dark-fearing child. It was long before they slept.

The office, next day, was a place of stark emotions As if it had finally become clear to everyone that the list of suspects was now very short indeed, eyes did not quite meet, and conversations were ended before they had properly begun. Coral did her work grimly, her voice bright with insincerity, tears not far away. Gwenny managed the switchboard without much success, her eyes red and nose perpetually sniffing with misery. The phones hardly stopped ringing, which was what Marius had expected; but it was none the less hard to put up with the constant enquiries, the press calls from just about everywhere, Montagu's angry agent from Philadelphia, and, yet again, 'Don Basilio' from Paris.

'I'm sorry,' Coral said, handing the phone to Marius. 'But she insists on speaking to you.'

'Hullo!' Marius said, his voice crisp and temper short.

After a long pause the voice came very clearly. 'Hi! Rhonda Sillitoe from Paris here. I'm calling Mary Hogbein…'

'The line is very good today,' Marius said with some penetration. 'Will you please pay attention to what I am about to say!'

'Time is money, my friend, especially at this distance. Can you get Ms Holbein?'

'Listen!' roared Marius out of his immense frustration. 'There is no Mary Hogbein. The person you want is *me*, Marius Hogbein! H-O-G-B-E-I-N! I am festival director...'

'I don't want to speak to the funeral director...'

'Madam!' Marius yelled. 'Can you stop talking long enough to listen? You have your facts wrong. It is MARIUS HOGBEIN you want. There *is* no Mary Hogbein. You have been misinformed. What information do you want?'

'You know,' said Ms Sillitoe coolly—clearly not a woman who was easily offended—'you are truly the rudest man I have ever spoken to. And that's really some accolade!'

'I shall *write* to you! Perhaps you would take the time to read! I suppose you can? Oh, yes, of course—you're a journalist, aren't you?' He leered dementedly down the phone. 'Meanwhile, Don Basilio, kindly do not ring me again!'

Just before he slammed the receiver down he heard the cool voice say, 'Don Basilio? Who the hell do you think is calling you? *Figaro*?'

He sat with the phone in his hand. 'She heard me! At last she heard me. Coral, don't ask me to speak to her again. Tell her—tell her I've been arrested...!'

Coral, who had begun to smile at the asinine conversation, pit her hand over her mouth and ran from the room, tears beginning to flow. 'Oh, damn!' Marius exploded. 'Oh, damn, damn, and damn it all to hell!' When he looked up, Nick Verdun was regarding him with a quizzical expression.

'May I come in?' Marius gestured wearily to a chair. 'You know, I do understand how stressful this must be for you, all of you. But please don't let it get to you. You'll all need each other when...'

'I know. What can I do for you?'

'I'd like to speak to Fletcher.'

'Be my guest.' He dared not ask why.

'Do you know where he is?'

'In his office, I imagine.'

'No. I've looked.' The tone of his voice made Marius look up sharply, and what he saw brought his heart into his mouth.

'He must be somewhere.' He called through the open door to Coral. 'Find Jim, will you, please?' While they waited he said cautiously, 'Developments?'

'Thoughts,' Verdun offered. 'I'm not getting much sleep, either.'

Briggs entered the room, and Verdun turned to him. 'Liaise with the others,' he said quietly. 'And let me know the moment they hear anything.' Marius longed to ask, but daren't. Briggs left. *To look for Jim?* Marius was thinking, wishing he hadn't imagined that.

Coral came back. 'He's not in the building.'

'Has he been in?'

'I haven't seen him myself.'

'Ring his home, Carol,' Marius said quietly, and she turned and went to her own desk.

Marius could not sit still. He stood by the window and stared blindly out, barely noticing the windsurfers scudding before the breeze, or the squadron of pelicans flapping majestically upstream. Verdun watched him without speaking. If the outcome of all this was to be as half expected it, Marius would need to be strong for the sake of his staff. As if he read the detective's mind, Marius turned.

'I'm not quite the lunatic I seem to be at the moment. If—*when* the blow comes, we shall all cope with it. Life goes on, doesn't it? I'm sure you've found in your line of business that when the chips are down people do somehow seem to make sense of it.'

Verdun nodded gravely. 'Resilience is one of the major human attributes. Otherwise we wouldn't make it.'

"What is so strange,' Marius murmured, 'is how soon we forget the people who were killed. That seemed the worst part of it at first…and now? They hardly get a mention.'

'It's a paradox,' Verdun agreed.

Coral came in. 'He isn't there.'

Taking a deep breath, Marius said, 'Get everyone in here, will you, please? Quickly.'

The office seemed crowded when everyone was assembled; yet there was a gap, clear to all: the gap that should have been filled by Jim Fletcher.

'Detective Sergeant Verdun wants to speak to Jim. Does anyone know where he is? Has he been in today?'

Eyes searched faces; but the answer was negative. Jim had not been seen. Verdun stood up.

'Thank you, Mr Hogbein,' he said formally, and nodded his appreciation to the rest of the staff. 'I'll be in touch.'

After he had left there was silence, and then a rush of sound as everyone spoke simultaneously. Marius looked from one to another, hoping for some sudden recollection, some hint of the young press officer's whereabouts; but it was clear that no one had any idea. He left the room, walked briskly through the hallway and out into the street, not knowing where he should go; and within him was growing a sensation of panic such as he had never experienced. On an impulse he spun round and ran to the car-park, wanting to get away, to have time to think, to prepare himself. If it was Jim...

Craig Schuster was standing beside Marius's car. 'Are you going to look for Jim?'

Marius shook his head. 'I wouldn't know where to start. That's Verdun's job.'

'I was—worried about you. I'm sorry. I shouldn't interfere. I just thought perhaps you would rush off and—and hit something. Your face, in there—it had me worried.' Craig's brow was creased, his eyes genuinely concerned. Marius put out a hand to him.

'Thank you. But you don't need to worry about me.' He glanced up at Craig while he was sliding into the driver's seat. 'Look after things for me for a while, will you, Craig? I need an hour or so off duty.'

'No worries!' Craig closed the door gently, bending down to wave, and Marius, as he swung the car out of the car-park, caught a glimpse of his face—a picture of anxious commiseration.

'How could it be Craig?' he was thinking as he drove, at first aimlessly, then with some purpose. 'Could he be so concerned, *and* a murderer? Or does it mean that Jim is the one, because he's disappeared? Could he be a victim? Oh, lord, I hope not! There's been enough...' He pulled into a circular driveway in front of an old, well-tended house in one of the more select neighbourhoods. As he walked up to the door and rang the bell he hoped that there would be someone at home.

Dame Clarissa opened the door to him herself. 'Marius!' she cried, clearly pleased to see him. 'What a wonderful surprise, dear boy!' She drew him in solicitously, sat him down, took one look at his face and poured him a brandy with a very little water. 'You are not well, Marius.'

'I'm well enough.' He drank the brandy too quickly and choked a little. 'Forgive me for coming. But I don't want to worry Alicia any more than I have to, and really there's no one else. Everyone else is too involved.'

'Sit! Relax! Rest!' She issued the commands and expected to be obeyed. She insisted on a footstool for his feet, another brandy when the first was finished, and soothing music on the record player. It was such a change of roles to be commanded, to relinquish the position of Lord High Everything, to lie back and not have to worry.

As he did so, eyes closed, the weariness and stress running out of him, Dame Clarissa allowed herself the rare delight of regarding him unseen. He was a good-looking man, but that wasn't the reason for her affection for him. Nor was it that he own son would have been about the same age if he had lived, though there might be something of that, too. It was a bond, a deep, heart-felt bond that she had recognised when she had first met him, when that idiot Beverly had been crowing about his own cleverness in getting this fine piece of property as their new festival director.

She had taken one look, and believed that here was someone who would be a real friend, almost like family; and when she had met his wife, Alicia, she had known that she was right. With these young people she could find a friendship of rare quality.

And so it had transpired. Now, as she watched him bowed by the weight of anxiety, she wanted to hold his hand, smooth his brow; but she knew that such familiarity would embarrass him. So she contented herself with regarding him as the colour came back into his face, and the eyes slowly opened and caught her watching him. He smiled sheepishly.

'You'll have to forgive me, Clarissa. It seems that one of my staff will be arrested for the murder, but I don't know which, and I don't know when.'

Dame Clarissa shook her head slowly, much grieved. 'My dear boy, how frightful for you. The sergeant is quite sure, I suppose?'

'I fear so.'

'And who does he…?' She paused delicately. Marius sat up and leaned forward, elbows on knees.

'Craig Schuster. Jim Fletcher. Clem Zacaria.'

Dame Clarissa snorted. 'Zacaria! What nonsense—the man's an idiot!'

'The man's an eccentric, Clarissa. Who knows what makes him tick? I don't! Unfortunately, something happened this morning… Jim hasn't come to work. No one knows where he is. I keep wondering—could he have taken off? Done a bunk? If not, what the hell does he think he's playing at? The man must be mad.'

'And Schuster?'

'I don't know. My mechanisms for recognising murderers are rusty!' He spoke with some bitterness. 'Craig's very controlled, not very forthcoming. But just now…' He told her about the meeting in the car-park. 'He sounded genuinely bothered about me. Could he be concerned, and still be the—the one? Is it possible?'

'I would imagine that where there is premeditated murder— and these must surely be premeditated?—there are no rules of behaviour. One must certainly be a little mad to perpetrate such… horrors?'

They were silent, companionably so; then Marius stirred. 'I must go back. Thank you for being soothing.' He managed a small smile. Dame Clarissa boomed a hearty laugh.

'I doubt if anyone has *ever* accused me of being soothing.'

'But you are. I feel soothed. I feel ready to go and start again.'

The old lady flushed with pleasure. 'In that case, we have mutually soothed each other. I'm glad you found it possible to come and share your—dilemma.' She stood, and he followed her to the door.' When this is all over, dear Marius, you and Alicia must come and spend a lovely evening with me. We shall forget the horrors, and I shall *not* invite poor old Beverly! I promise.'

So they were able to laugh as they parted, and Marius returned to the office refreshed and strengthened. Dame Clarissa closed the door behind her and stood for a moment, head high and a pink residue in her wrinkled cheeks. He must not be worried more than needful. If necessary, she would have to lay down the law.

21

Mave, entering her bank, met Sir Beverly coming out. If she had not been deep in thought she would have seen him, but it was too late. 'Ah!' said that gentleman, and gave her what might almost be called a courtly bow.

'Sir Beverly!' she acknowledged, and tried to pass.

'Goin' anywhere special?' he asked, all gross charm. She thought quickly, but not quickly enough for the importunate knight. 'Take time off and have a cup of coffee with a lonely old man!' He managed to sound at once ingratiating and pathetic. Mave groaned inwardly.

'I really can't, Sir Beverly. I have a great deal of work…'

'Ah-ha! You know what they say? All work and no play makes *Mave* a dull girl!'

'How his compliments are laced with implied insults,' she thought, feeling trapped. 'Well—just half an hour,' she said grudgingly. 'I do have work to do.'

'I'll wait for you here.' He sat down, huge and dauntingly visible, on a rather small sofa of the kind that banks favour. She went to the counter and transacted her business with the teller, all the time wondering if there was an escape route.

'Do you have a back way out?' she asked the surprised girl, who shook her head as she counted out the notes.

'Where did you want to get to?'

'Freedom,' said Mave enigmatically, and bowed to the inevitable.

Over the coffee he managed to make himself quite amiable. Mave, no shrinking violet herself, was less put out by his thundering delivery of trite conversation than a more delicate woman might have been. All the same, his determination to deal in intimate details and dissections of the city's better-known personalities (while enchanting for any journalist to hear) was somewhat embarrassing. Suddenly, as if his mind had finally homed in on its target, he said, 'Thought any more about my offer?'

Mave had to think for a moment. For *offer* read *proposition*? 'I don't think we have anything to discuss on that score,' she said, as kindly as possible considering the high decibel count required to deliver the message to its destination.

'Oh, come!' he retorted, jocular as ever. 'Not a bad idea, if you think about it. Wouldn't *bother* you too much—y'know what I mean? Past most o' that these days. Companionship, that's what it's all about. Someone to talk to. Someone who cares whether you're comfortable—that kind of thing. Bears thinking about.'

He gave her a smile of great warmth that frightened her more than all the blustering could have done. He was obviously entirely serious about it.

'I've been on my own a long time, Beverly. I like my freedom. I enjoy running my own life without having to trim it to fit someone else's. I have no wish to find myself part of a *couple* again. Can't you understand?'

He was hearing her remarkably well this morning. He gave her that wide, sickening smile again, clearly enjoying the strength of his emotions for her. 'Have another coffee, little lady,' he said in low, intimate tones, as if that would solve everything. He waved to the waitress. 'We'll talk about this again, my dear.'

'No, we won't!' Mave said crisply. She was aware of interested faces at nearby tables, but she couldn't help that. These were desperate times. 'We have nothing at all to say to each other on this matter, Sir Beverly. Nothing at all. I'm sorry, but there it is.'

He leered at her again. 'But I thought you rather liked me,' he said coyly. He reached out and tried to take her hand, but she pulled back sharply. Even that didn't stop him. It was obvious he had read the books that say that when a woman says 'no', she means 'yes'.

'I like you. Of course I do. But that doesn't mean marriage.' She regretted her cowardice; she should make it clear that he was abhorrent to her. Four pairs of eyes at the nearest table were glued on her, and she glared back. 'I am not in the marriage market, Sir Beverly. *Not—in—the—marriage—market!*' She enunciated very clearly.

At last he leaned back, not in the manner of a man giving up the chase, but rather as a big-game hunter might take time to recharge his rifle. Not in the least disturbed, he changed the subject.

'This Vaughan feller got the murders tied up yet, has he?'

Mave blinked. 'Not as far as I know.'

'Rotten business. Should never have happened. Police force needs a good shake-up. Letters to the papers. Royal Commission! External investigations. Should have solved it days ago. This feller Vardon's obviously no damn good. Put him back on the beat! I'll see the Commissioner myself.'

'I suppose,' Mave said carefully, not wanting to get caught in another fortissimo argument, 'that they have to have proof— evidence. Before they can make an arrest.'

'Proof? Garbage! Take 'em all in and put pressure on 'em! Can't afford to treat 'em with kid gloves. A few nights in the cells on bread and water, that's what it wants!'

Mave stared at him, wondering what system of justice had produced him. 'I think you would find that Sergeant Verdun's hands are tied by the democratic principles of our judicial system.'

The old man snorted. 'Democratic! Hah! Mealy-mouthed puling, that's what it is. Need a strong hand. If I'd been in charge of this investigation we'd have had someone under lock and key by now!'

'The guilty person?' Mave asked sweetly, gathering her impedimenta about her ready for a quick getaway. 'Or just someone to fill a cell?'

Sir Beverly struggled to his feet as she stood and made clear her intention to leave. 'I say, goin' already? Well, think over what I've been saying. Loneliness is not good for man nor beast. Let me know.'

Outside the café, Mave stopped for a moment to draw a long breath free of Beverly's accumulated tobacco odour. She wondered briefly about emigration. Wondered why three exemplary musicians should have been sacrificed when there was a splendid victim all ready for dispatch in the awful knight. She shook herself, mentally and physically.

'He's just an old man,' she assured herself, 'revolting, but harmless. Just take care he doesn't catch you when you've had one too much and your guard's down.'

But as she walked away to her next morning chore she found herself pondering once more on the fate of their murderer. Who? Why? How? She was glad she wasn't Nick Verdun.

Marius was at the airport. So were Alicia, Detective Sergeant Verdun, an assorted posse of police who presumably felt that they were part of the background scenery; and Charles Pegler and Alan Corelli, standing sadly by the departure lounge doors, waiting to take off for the States and a new future without Montagu Brammar. Not that they would be far from him for the next few hours; out on the tarmac the coffin was already being loaded into the bowels of the aircraft.

'Well,' Marius said, because there was so little one could say at a time like this. He held out his hand, a lump in his throat making it hard to express himself effectively. Alicia managed it better, putting her arms around the two men and allowing them to hug her before standing back and smiling an admittedly watery smile.

'It is a tragedy,' Alan said. 'Of course! But we shall have to get on without the man somehow. We seriously thought of fulfilling our commitments in other states by finding a temporary replacement for Monty. But it would have been hard, very hard, to play these works without him. One day! But not just yet.'

Charles sighed. 'I'm grieved for you, Marius. This will take a heap of getting over, getting back to normal. I don't know how you've coped.'

'I haven't,' said Marius with simplicity. 'Once the Bach B minor is over I shall be hard put not to sink without trace.'

'We weren't able to say goodbye to your staff,' Alan said after a pause. 'It seemed best not to, under the circumstances.'

'Of course.' Marius understood completely. Until they knew who was the murderer they could hardly be expected to thank anyone for what should have been a rewarding visit. The remembrance of a splendid recital had long since been lost under the traumas that had followed.

They stood, conversation dwindling to nothing; then Alan made a move, catching Charles's eye, and the group moved towards the doors. Verdun, after shaking hands with the two Americans, stood back and let the Hogbeins make their final farewells.

As they turned to leave, he re-joined them. Marius, his face drawn, suddenly said, 'Whatever happened to Tiger-Kitten?' Verdun wondered momentarily whom he meant, then smiled.

'The Lady Tabitha? I let her go. She was off like a startled rabbit, probably to pastures new. Not much will faze that young lady. Why do you ask?'

Marius shrugged. 'I'd completely forgotten about her. I suppose she was never really likely to be a suspect, was she? Not being here for the first one. But I should have checked up on her—see if she was all right.'

'Oh, she was all right! She had a go at one of my young men, but I soon stopped that. Then she said she was off, and I saw no reason to hold her for suspicion. Not suspicion of murder, anyway!' He grinned suddenly, and Marius, in spite of his dour mood, grinned back. Alicia raised her eyebrows in mock disapproval.

'Men! Throw you a pair of long legs and everything else falls into place.'

Marius took her hand. 'The price of a virtuous woman is above rubies,' he said piously, and she glanced at him with a wry smile.

'And what is the price of a virtuous man, if such could be found?'

'A carton of beer!' said Marius, and hurried her to the car.

When Verdun arrived back in his office there was a note for him. Country police had located Jim Fletcher's car, travelling southward, and had stopped it. Jim had been much surprised, it seemed. And when they insisted that he should travel with them to the city, there to be closely questioned about his defection, he turned very pale and had to sit down.

'I don't see why,' he said.

'Further enquiries into the murder of...' began the country policeman.

Jim waved an arm limply. 'All right, I know, I know...' he looked from one to the other of the officers. 'But it wasn't me. I didn't do it.'

'You can tell Sergeant Verdun that when you get there.' They bundled him into the police car and began to run back.

'What about my car?' Jim exclaimed, turning round to see it disappear in a puff of road dust.

'It'll be kept at the police station until it's claimed.'

'Oh, my God!' Jim put his head in his hands. 'Am I under arrest?'

'You're helping us with our enquiries, technically speaking.'

Jim slumped. 'I didn't think...'

'Most people don't, sir,' the driver said stolidly, and they sped on, decorously but horribly inevitably, on the road back to town.

Verdun met him with chilling courtesy. He showed him into an interview room and sat down opposite him with that steely look in his eye. Jim was getting to know the look.

'Well, Mr Fletcher! You took off without letting me know where you were going. So I must ask you to fill me in. You were requested to keep in touch.'

'*I* wasn't told I couldn't leave town,' Jim said with a sudden spurt of annoyance. 'You never told me that.'

'So where were you going?'

'Down to Bridgefield. To see my fiancée. I don't know where she is—I've tried phoning. After the other night when she rang me and couldn't get through…well, I've been worried. I thought I'd go and see for myself.' He stared miserably across the desk at Verdun. 'Perhaps I shouldn't have gone, but it doesn't mean that I'm a—a murderer!' He stopped suddenly. 'I don't want her to worry about me. She's a very *gentle* person. Not like city girls.'

'What a dear old-fashioned thing he is!' Verdun thought. He certainly didn't look like a murderer—not at this moment, with his hair standing on end and his face pallid and drawn. 'You can go,' he said. 'But I must insist that you let me know if you are going outside the metropolitan boundaries.'

Jim stood slowly, looking down at him. 'You're still not sure, then?' He gave a short, almost angry laugh. 'I just hope you find out who did it very soon. This is a frightful situation for an innocent man to be in.'

He left the room, and young Briggs watched him go. 'Any nearer to knowing, Sarge?' he asked, and Verdun nodded slowly.

'Yes, it's coming together. It's a matter of motive, Briggs. We need to know *why*. You see…' He began to talk, and Briggs listened with interest. After he had filled the constable in on some of his theories, he wrote swiftly on a pad and tore off the sheet. 'I want you to find out for me…' Briggs was nodding slowly, still without quite understanding. 'The quicker the better!'

Briggs left. Verdun sat for a moment as if weary. Much as he wished to close the case, he feared the outcome for people he had come to regard almost as friends. He pulled the pad closer and began to write. There was little doubt in his mind now, but he needed hard evidence. And once he had that…it would be over.

The door flew open and a young woman stood just inside the room and glared at Marius. Taken by surprise, he stood up. 'Where's Jim?' the girl demanded. 'Whatever's going on here?'

'You're Mary,' Marius said, relieved. 'Of course! Where have you been?'

'Where have *I* been?' She stared at him, eyes wide. 'I've been visiting my mother in hospital. And suddenly I hear that Jim's arrested. For what? What's he done?'

Marius gestured towards a chair and called for Carol to make two cups of coffee. 'Or tea, if you'd rather?'

Mary shook her head impatiently. 'Whatever you're having. So where is Jim now?'

'I don't know. Not at this exact moment.'

'With the police?'

'No. They let him go.'

'And so I should jolly well think!' She was beautifully irate. 'What lumbering idiot could think that *Jim*, of all people…?'

'Mary…' Marius held her eyes with his. 'Mary, *someone* did these murders. And it was someone associated with the festival— we know that. So it narrows the field. Much as I like Jim, I can't pretend that he is yet in the clear in the eyes of the police. It was extremely foolish of him to go haring off south like he did. It was bound to look like a break. Can you see?' He paused, wondering if she understood. 'Before long, one of us *is* going to be arrested for three senseless, ugly killings. I don't see how *any* of my young people could be involved. But I think one of them must be. That is the hard truth we have had to face these past days.'

Mary regarded him solemnly, her eyes distressed. 'I hadn't realised. How awful for you.'

He nodded, trying to smile. 'Yes, it is. It's awful! I keep hoping the—the person will come forward and confess, take this pressure off the rest of us. But since the pattern of thinking of this killer is something beyond my own comprehension I have to say that I cannot see anything but an agonising outcome. We are all on edge. You must forgive us.'

'Can I see Jim?'

'If you can find him. He mustn't leave the city without telling the police.'

'So they obviously think he could have done it?'

'The suspects are Jim, Craig and Clem Zacaria. I think it's all right to tell you. We all realise…Everyone else was accounted for when the last murder took place. But Jim was out of the lounge, trying to reach you on the phone…'

'Trying to reach me?'

He nodded. 'And Craig—well, I'm not sure where Craig was. Clem Zacaria came in after the shot was fired. So he's not in the clear yet, either. But the rest of us were in the lounge, at the reception. Unless someone totally not associated with the festival is involved, that's the state of things.'

'And couldn't it be someone outside? Why must it be one of you?'

'Hardly anyone knew where Signor Alessandri was when he was killed. That cut the number of suspects down considerably.'

She sat, deep in thought. 'What a mess! Well, I'll see if I can find Jim. Poor love! He must be wondering what's hit him.' As she went towards the door she stopped. '*When* was he trying to phone me?'

'On that night—when Montagu Brammar was shot. As I recall it, he was told there was a phone call from you, but when he went upstairs to take it the line was dead. So he tried to ring you. But he couldn't get through. So then he went outside to a call-box nearby and tried again. But you were out. Or so he thought. He wanted to reassure you—that he wasn't in any danger from this—mass-murderer. When he couldn't get you he came back to the reception, to find that there had been another shooting.'

Mary was looking puzzled. 'This was the night of Mr Brammar's murder? I don't understand. *I* didn't try to ring him that night. You see,' she turned and came back to the desk, 'my mother had a heart attack that morning, and Dad and I were with her all day at the hospital. They thought at one time she might not make it. So, of course, we were totally wrapped up in what was happening to her. By about eleven I suddenly thought about Jim, but it was too late to ring. Besides, I knew he was worried about the situation here. I didn't want to pile anything more on him.' She gave a small smile. 'He's very fond of my mother. Then the following morning she was very up and down, and by the time I got to a phone he had left home. I nearly rang him here, then thought I wouldn't. It's not as if it was urgent by that time. And my thoughts were more with Mum.'

'I can understand that. How is she now?'

Mary took a deep breath and crossed her fingers. 'Good, we hope. She's been lucky.'

Marius frowned suddenly. 'How did you know about Jim?'

A fine worry line appeared between her eyes. 'That's odd, under the circumstances. A message by phone. My father answered it, just before breakfast this morning. A man said that Jim had been arrested, and I should ring the local police. No name! And he rang off without speaking to me. Just "Jim has been arrested", and put the receiver down. I didn't have time to think about it. I rang the police and they told me what had happened.' She stopped. 'Do you know, I'm feeling very angry about all this! What do you suppose is going on?'

Marius took a deep breath to steady his pounding heart. 'I think perhaps the murderer rang you. I don't know why. But I can't think who else it could have been. The police would have introduced themselves properly.'

'Oh, God!' she whispered, hands to mouth. 'Why would he do a thing like that?'

Marius lifted his phone. 'We'll get round to see Sergeant Verdun. He needs to know about this.'

22

Mary sat herself down on the front steps of Jim's unit, determined to be there when he eventually returned home. It was a longish wait. Had she known it, she could have cut the time by a couple of hours. But there was no way she could know that he was sitting in the small coffee shop just around the corner, tucked away in the back behind a room divider so that no one would see him, and he would have time to think.

The business with the police had shaken him badly. Suddenly, perhaps for the first time, he realised what he was up against. Plenty of people must have gone through the same situation; many, rightly or wrongly, would have been accused and found guilty. There were documented cases—he had read of them—where men had been hanged in the old days for murders which, later, had been proved to have been done by someone else. His stomach ached at the thought.

It would not be enough to say that he was innocent and therefore they couldn't prove him guilty. Innocent until the opposite was proved! Yet things could and did go wrong. He bought another cup of coffee and stared down into its murky depths, trying to recall all he knew about the three murdered pianists. But his mind rejected it. He had already told Verdun that he didn't move in those circles socially, even if his work brought him into professional contact with them. He groaned silently, and wished he could talk to Mary. Where could she be?

The coffee was cold, and this was getting him nowhere. Action was called for, proper, constructive thought; and as a start he would go and try to ring her once more. Energised by his sudden decision, he left the coffee shop and ran the short distance home.

'*There* you are!' said Mary. 'Poor lad—wherever have you been?' In his euphoria at seeing her, Jim slipped and fell, bruising his knee and grazing a hand. But the pain went unnoticed; he threw his arms around her and held her close.

'Where have *I* been?' he said at last through her hair. 'I've nearly gone mad trying to ring you. What happened?'

'Inside!' she said, leading him to the door. 'And I'll tell you everything.' She looked at him closely, seeing the pale face, the rings around the eyes. 'You really do need someone to look after you, don't you?' As she closed the door behind him he nodded passionately.

'Oh, yes! Yes, please!' He pulled her to him and held her desperately; she could sense his confusion.

'Come on, love,' she said gently, and led him to the elderly sofa. 'Sit down and tell me all about it.'

It was not a pretty tale, she decided. She couldn't blame the police; they had a job to do, and part of it was to protect the public. But anyone who knew Jim—'Oh, it's ridiculous!' she exclaimed as he told her about the police nabbing him that morning. 'You couldn't hurt as fly, James Fletcher!'

'Tell that to the fuzz.' He managed a pale grin. But when he heard about the telephone call that had not emanated from Mary on that fateful night, and the more recent call that morning, taken by her father, his face grew grim.

'I don't like it, Mary.' His voice was tense. 'Am I being framed? And if so—who?' They stared at each other in silence. This was a whole new departure; there was an element of evil in it beyond what had already been shown in the brutal, senseless shootings.

After a while he turned to search her face with worried eyes. 'Are you staying?' he asked, tentative, almost shy; and she nodded firmly. He sighed, relieved. 'Thank God! I don't want to be alone.'

She smiled gently at him. 'I see no reason why we should either of us be alone, ever again,' she said; and when he had taken her meaning he put his arms around her once more and buried his face in her hair.

'You don't think I could have possibly done these things, do you?' he said, his voice muffled, and she took the question seriously.

'Never! Not in a million years. You couldn't, Jim. I know it.'

'Then I can take whatever comes.' He felt certainty growing within him. 'They say it's an ill wind...'

'I need to find the gun,' Verdun was saying to his team. 'I may not need it as evidence, but you can't have too much of that. Besides, it'll leave a loose end. So we shall need to search the festival offices again, very thoroughly, and the ballet company offices, and the private homes of certain people. OK, Briggs?' Briggs nodded, making more notes. 'I'll have the necessary paperwork done by late afternoon, and then you can go to work.'

'Do you think we'll find it?'

'I doubt it, as a matter of fact. We haven't managed to locate it so far, and I can't see why it wouldn't have been disposed of after the third murder. But you never know.'

'Are we expecting more shootings, Sarge?'

He grinned at the young constable, grimly. 'I *always* expect shooting—or something—you know that. As a result, I'm usually pleasantly surprised when there isn't anything.' Then he grew properly solemn again. 'I think it's over. Whatever the reasons for the killings, they seem to have been associated with international pianists, and there are no more coming here for a couple of months. If we haven't broken it by then, of course, we shall have to think again. But my gut feeling is that it's over now. Let's pray it is.'

As the team left the room he returned to his desk. There was a faxed message there, with information that gave a glimmer of light. He stood, looking down at the words that made the difference between day and night in this strangely ephemeral case. He could not recall a case for a long time in which there seemed so little rhyme or reason—random killings with just that one strange link: the profession of the slain musicians.

'...*the death*' he read on the typed report, '*was apparently accidental, though further investigation revealed a suspected, or rumoured, connection between the dead person and your victim...*' Verdun hoped that it would show enough light to illumine the evil that had been perpetrated in these last weeks.

'An important job for you,' he said to Briggs, who had remained behind. The constable jumped up, ready and willing. 'Two coffees, two hamburgers with all the trimmings, and one of those little custard things in a plastic whatsit for me.' He fished money out of his pocket. 'Here...make it sharp. I'm hungry!'

Hal Princeton was looking very ill. Certainly Mave thought so, looking across the lunch table at him; Hal, catching sight of himself in the mirror this morning, had felt distinctly distressed at the thought that this unsavoury creature was the alcoholic Hal Princeton with whom he, often unwillingly, shared this same ailing body. He felt so sick that he had not smoked a cigar for twenty-four hours, and sometimes thought he never would again. That was how bad it was!

'What am I going to do with you, silly man?' Mave said, crossly but not without affection. 'Have you been to the doctor?'

He pulled a face. 'Have pity, Mave! What have I got to show to a quack that he hasn't seen a million times before?'

'I wasn't thinking of anything unique,' she said with due sarcasm, knowing that it was expected of her. 'Just a boring old case of an elderly fool who won't stop destroying himself.' She picked up the menu. 'What's it to be? Good, nourishing broth? A nice piece of grilled fish?'

Hal drew his breath shallowly. 'I know you mean to help, Mave,' he began, then coughing took over, and he emerged from the bout with red patches on his cheeks and a whistling breath that indicated more than she liked to think of. She put the menu down and advanced her face at him across the table, her over-made-up eyes full of angry compassion.

'You are sick, Hal! Sick! When are you going to admit defeat and go for help?'

'I'm too busy just now.'

'Busy?' She snorted. 'Doing what?'

'There is no reason to be offensive,' he said with some dignity. 'There is the Bach tomorrow night. I must be there…'

'Why? Can't they do it without you?'

He drew himself up. 'The review is an important part of the performance. It is an evaluation, a commendation if the performance has been good, a gentle reproof if not. It is a rounding off of all the work that has gone into it, an accolade sometimes, a moment on the day after when the participants sit down and read an informed judgement on something to which they may have been too close for proper evaluation.'

'You take yourself very seriously, old boy.' He glared at her, but the arrival of the waitress precluded the throwing of insults. He drew back into himself.

Once the food was on the table they relaxed, abandoning the sharp witticisms. Mave looked up at him, jangling her bracelets up her arm as she lifted her fork. 'Whatever made you become a critic, anyway?' She was taken aback by the complex emotions suddenly revealed on his sallow face. 'What did you do before?'

There was a long moment before he answered. 'I had the knowledge. I was interested. I had a pension…'

'A pension?'

He hesitated. 'Army. Invalided out. A pension meant I didn't have to teach, or do any of the things I wasn't fitted for. I came here…'

'When?'

'Fifty-seven.'

'Korean war, then?' She watched him curiously. He nodded, pushing the food around his plate aimlessly.

'When I came out of hospital I wasn't sure what to do…'

'What had you done before?'

Unexpectedly he looked up, as if he needed to see her reaction to what he was saying. 'I was a concert pianist,' he said simply.

Mave stopped eating. 'A good one?'

He shrugged. 'So they said. I was told I would go far.' He paused. 'I did. I went to Korea!' It was a pale enough jest. But she creased a smile at him briefly.

'What happened? Did you damage your hands?'

He put down his fork and held his hands up, first one way then the other. 'Not a scar! Not a cut or bruise. Just...when I came out they wouldn't play anymore.'

'Shell-shock or whatever they call it these days?'

'Mental breakdown, they called it. They got me back on my feet again, gave me a life to live, paid me a pension for having failed to come out a hero. But they were never able to give me back my hands.' He regarded them thoughtfully, as if he had never seen them before. 'They're quite nice hands, aren't they? But useless for the purpose God devised them for. No more piano playing! No more touring or promenade concerts or broadcasts or recording sessions. But perhaps there has been something worth doing. Perhaps I have helped to guide public opinion, just a little. Do you think so?' He gave her a quirky, heart-broken glance, and she reached out and took one of those 'useless' hands lying before her on the table.

'I never knew,' she said in a voice more gentle, more comfortable, than she would normally allow to escape her. 'Why have you never told me?'

He shrugged again. 'Who needs to know? Who wants hearts and flowers? If you're mad enough to go off and fight a war you stopped believing in, in a country you never wanted to visit anyway, I reckon you've got it coming to you. Don't you?'

He looked so drawn, so dejected, that her heart went out to him. 'I'm going to get you home,' she said with determination. 'And you can review the Bach. But after that it's the doctor for you, my boy. Don't bother to argue. Mother knows best!'

It was a measure of his weakness that he let her settle the bill and call a taxi to deposit them at his front door. Once inside, she made him sit down and put a stool under his feet. His head was dry and warm—to his disgust she felt it with her own dry, warm hand. She had intended to leave him. But there was washing up to be done; the bed had not been made. Knowing his usual pernickety neatness, she wondered. He was not a man to live in a pig-sty. As she pottered she fancied he dozed now and again; and in the quiet room she found herself being drawn back to the recent tragedies, and to the possible outcome. Would a man so resent the career of a successful pianist that...? She shuddered.

'Who *did* do it, Hal, do you suppose?' But he snored gently; and after a while, seeing him comfortable, she crept away and left him.

23

Marius had called in during the afternoon to see how the big rehearsal was going. The replacement bass was singing as he arrived, halfway through the lovely *Et in Spiritum Sanctum*, his voice fluid and unstressed. Marius sat down at the back of the hall to listen to the following chorus, and then that noble, majestic *Sanctus*, full of a wonderful vitality, the splendid triplets sweeping it along and up to the crisp rhythm of the *Pleni sunt*, women's voices running in thirds towards its triumphant conclusion.

Such energy old Bach had; that paterfamilias whose sons had little time for him musically, the one they called 'the old peruke'— an anachronism, a has-been. But he had outlived them all! Good as the next generation was, Old Bach would never die as long as there were musicians who believed that music was yet another and glorious way of harnessing energy.

He left the hall on more of a cloud of pleasure than he had known for days. Too often lately the cloud had been on top, and its underbelly was grey and threatening.

Verdun was in the office when he returned, which was one good way of popping his bubble of well-being. The warrants were there, the police had power to search again where they would. He sat down, feeling a little sick. In a community such as this one, where they were careful of each other's privacy and feelings, it seemed diabolical to let strangers, young, impersonal strangers, go through private drawers, cupboards, boxes. But it had to be done. He flung open his own drawers with a kind of dramatic abandon.

'Go for your life! You *still* won't find anything.'

They were thorough, probably more so than the first time. And they were certainly impersonal. On second thoughts he was glad that it was so. It would have been insufferable if, by even a glint in the eye, they had revealed amusement at Gwenny's little album of rock stars' autographs, or Coral's toilet bag tucked away at the back of her drawer.

Craig Schuster, shrugging, wandered out into the garden while the search was on, standing with legs apart, relaxed, gazing at the river where tourist cruisers were beginning to come home from their day out. When Verdun let him know that they had finished with his belongings he came in again, nodding quite coolly, not at all dismayed. Marius wondered if that was a good sign or a bad one.

'Are you searching anywhere else, or are we the lucky ones?' he asked Verdun, who was watching his men as they failed to turn up anything of value.

'We've already been over the ballet company. Zacaria was fairly livid about it, but we didn't find anything.'

'And do you expect to find anything here?'

Verdun turned an enigmatic expression on him. '*Should* we? It has to be done. You know that.'

Marius watched silently. 'Are you coming to the concert tonight? I have a ticket for you if you want.'

The sergeant hesitated. 'My men will be there.' He made a sudden decision. 'Yes, thank you. I'll come. If I don't I shall be wondering all evening...'

'If someone's getting shot?'

Verdun grinned. 'No. What it is about this music that gets so many people together. I thought Australia was a sporting nation.'

Marius offered a grimace that had to do for a smile. 'I believe some do play sport,' he conceded. 'But this is where the real action is!'

There is a distinct difference between a comfortably full hall and a complete sell-out. The atmosphere can be felt even before entering the auditorium. On this night Marius lifted his nose to the ambience of the place, like a gun dog to the scent. A crowded hall, a superb work, top class performers—what else could he ask for as the culmination of his festival? Perhaps only the more plebeian pleasures of the fireworks after the show!

It was another night to remember in this period when stark tragedy had been interspersed with fine cultural achievements. He had no reason to feel badly; he had done his work, and if someone had seen fit to use it as the background to an orgy of killing, he could not be held to blame. Next year...! It was the first time in days he had been able to contemplate taking up this particular burden and beginning all over again. His spirits were rising.

From where he was sitting, in a side box, he could see Jim and Mary down in the stalls, Craig across from him in another box. Verdun was somewhere towards the back, a placing which didn't matter on a night when the music would fill every available space, pouring into and around and beneath each raptly listening member of the audience. He wondered what the detective would make of the massive work.

Sir Beverly was in the next box with Dame Clarissa; he seemed less bumptious than usual. Perhaps the old lady had read him the Riot Act, or maybe he was simply growing older gracefully—at last. Hal Princeton, looking quite ghastly from above, was in the stalls, pen and notebook at the ready. Mave Cardwell was there, too, somewhere. Ah, there! draped in something long and gold and eye-catching, her eyes dark with too much mascara, that black hair grotesque above a face powdered beyond endurance.

He could see so many old faithfuls, regulars who came year after year, never missing until frailty or death overcame them. He must be doing something right, he told himself; and took Alicia's hand in his for additional comfort.

The concertmaster came on, and then the soloists and the conductor. And the world faded into insignificance under the spell of timeless music.

24

'A-ha! What did you think of that, eh, Yale?' Sir Beverly poked Hal in the midriff, spilling some of the wine from his own glass as he did so. Bach was over; this was winding-down time, the end-of-festival reception.

'Very fond of Bach, as you know, Sir Beverly. A fine performance.'

'Going to give it a good write-up, are you? Better than all that modern crap. Wouldn't you say, Yale? You can't actually enjoy those cat-noises. Eh, Yale?' He gave an explosive laugh. 'You see, I've got it right this time, eh, eh? Yale, like the lock. Always have difficulty with names, but the trick is to find something that reminds you. Always thought of Yankee colleges before. But I've got it this time. Yale, like the lock.' He nodded, satisfied. Hal stared at him wanly.

'Princeton,' he said, with patience he didn't feel. '*Princeton!* Not that it matters.'

But Sir Beverly had stopped listening.

'I was hoping that once the Bach was over we could relax,' Marius said. 'I suppose I thought that this mess would all be cleared up simultaneously with the end of the festival. I was wrong.'

Alicia was brushing her hair. It was very late, but it had been a good evening, rounding off the weeks of festivity very satisfyingly.

Marius, his shirt hanging open, was wandering round the bedroom aimlessly, his 'high' slowly descending to normal.

'I had hoped we could go away—straight off! Anywhere! Just for a few days of peace and quiet.'

'Me, too.' Alicia's eye was on him as he perambulated. He took off a sock and looked for somewhere to drop it, finally leaving it in the middle of the sheepskin rug.

'But I can't go anywhere until the—the case is finalised.'

'Of course.'

'You do understand, don't you?' She nodded at him, yawning a little. 'It's very annoying, I know. But it's out of my hands. If—*when* Verdun wraps it up we're likely to have a fair amount of emotional clearing up to do. Coral's been great, but it's all taken its toll. Gwenny's been crying for about three weeks.'

'Poor Gwenny.' She slipped off her negligée, climbed into bed. 'How near is the sergeant to completing it?' Neither of them could use the real words, the forbidden words: 'murder', 'arrest', 'trial'. Euphemisms held sway.

'I don't know. Sometimes I think he's got it all sorted out, but then I wonder. Surely he would—complete it, if he had the evidence?'

'That's probably it. He needs to have evidence.'

Marius put on his pyjama jacket and looked around vaguely for the matching shorts. Alicia threw them to him from the bed. He pulled them on, then sat down on the edge of the mattress, his attention off somewhere she could not follow.

'Come to bed,' she said. 'You've had enough. When Verdun does—what he has to do, you'll need all your strength. They'll be relying on you.'

He lifted the quilt and slid under. 'I know. I think that's what terrifies me. I'm so tired. Oh, Alicia, I'm so very tired.'

She switched off the bedside light and pulled him to her. For a while he was rigid, lying against her with every muscle tense, unable to relax. Then, 'But the Bach was good, wasn't it? At least, the Bach was good.' When he turned towards her and put his face against her shoulder, she felt his tears.

When Hal had finished writing his review and rung it in to the newspaper, Mave decided that the time had come for some straight talking. And she talked straight, for several minutes in a bar they both knew, until it dawned on her that he wasn't listening. The stimulus of a really good concert had brought hectic colour to his face; but he still looked like a scarecrow, a gaunt figure of despair. He was drinking steadily, and she wanted him to stop, because she knew he was destroying himself; and yet she didn't want to stop him, because now, after his revelations of the previous night, she knew that forgetfulness was his only comfort.

So she called a cab ('what I spend on taxis for you!' she exclaimed in feigned irritation), and took him home, settling him in his chair and trying not to watch him slowly disintegrating. 'I could cry!' she told herself; but crying was really not her style.

'D'you think they'll ever sort out these murders?' she asked him, endeavouring to keep him in touch with reality. 'This Verdun—if he going to win, do you think?'

Hal stared at her lugubriously. 'There'sh and great deal of e-evil in the world,' he said with commendable clarity. 'The poleesh-police are the vacu-u-um cleaners of society. Into their dusht-proof bag goesh all the—the evil and the filth and the...' He lost his thread and took another sip instead.

'That's an interesting metaphor,' Mave said. 'Or is it a simile? I can never remember.'

'Evil thingsh have been done,' he went on with the measured pronunciation of the well-drunk. 'And retribu-bution will follow. As sure as my name'sh...' he giggled suddenly, 'Yale! Bloody stupid old man!' Mave didn't need to ask who; they were her sentiments exactly.

'Why is it taking so long?' Mave said, more to herself than to Hal, who was singing—if that was the word for it—the resounding phrases of the *Sanctus*. 'Is it really such a difficult case to crack? Let's see!' She sat down an Hal's bottle-cluttered table and stared ahead of her at an oil landscape of Ayers Rock, gaudily daubed in shades of purple and crimson as the sun went down. 'Who did this offensive painting?'

Hal turned his head painfully to see. 'Don't mock a man's secret passion. *I* did it.'

Mave snorted. 'I had no idea you were an artist.' She put her head on one side to see if the picture looked any better that way. It didn't. 'You should have taken lessons.' But her attention wandered back to the murders. Like the Rock, they could not be ignored; and if the crimes were luridly purple and crimson, then all the more reason for getting them out of the way so that they could all get on with living again. 'What are the main points? What has Verdun been looking at? What does he hope to find?'

She made them cups of coffee, which Hal did not touch, and then she sat down again, going over the details of the case, wondering out loud and getting little response from her companion. 'But what's the *link*?' She said at last. She clasped her head in her hands, bangles rattling like curtain rings along her arms. 'Where's the *connection*? In God's name—*where is the connection?'* Hal sang a plaintive snatch of Bach, his eyes half-closed against the light.

'Three pianists,' she said, going back to the beginning. 'Three *international* pianists. But no point of contact. They didn't even know each other.'

'Three pianishts,' Hal said helpfully.

Mave glared at him. 'Or three drum majorettes! Or three bakers! So what? If there's no connection…' She stopped, staring at the awful painting, seeing it yet not seeing it. 'A glimmer!' she said softly. 'I believe I see a glimmer. Hal!' She turned slowly towards him, noting the glazed eyes, the puffy cheeks. 'Hal, old friend, you are killing yourself. Do you know that?' Unexpectedly she felt tears prickle behind the mascara. 'Listen to me now, you silly man! Where would you hide a bottle?'

'I don'—don't hide bottlesh…' he said with sozzled dignity.

'But if you did, would you hide it on a glass-topped table? In the middle of the road?' She leaned over to shake his arm. 'In a bowling alley? Hal—where would you hide a bottle?'

He opened his eyes, rubbed his face, puzzled. 'Behind the clock?' he said at last.

'No, you silly fool! No!' She stared into his eyes triumphantly. *'You'd hide it in a wine cellar!'* She laughed suddenly. 'In a wine cellar, you sozzled old dear!' Hal gazed at her blankly. 'And where would you hide a murder?' she asked, her voice suddenly soft. 'You'd hide it in a *collection* of murders. That's the answer, old pal. *There is no connection between these murders!* There's one murder— and two pieces of camouflage. Why didn't I see it before?'

She leaned back, great excitement running through her, spiritual adrenalin. Throwing her head back she laughed silently, amazed at her own perspicacity. 'Oh, Hal, boy, there's life in the old bitch yet!'

He gave a sudden snore and the glass fell from his hand. Mave picked it up, hardly conscious of what she was doing. 'But which one?' she asked herself urgently. 'Which is *the* murder? Which are the decoys?'

Hal surfaced for a moment from a sea of spirituous fumes. 'Why did you put your bottle in the mid-middle of the road?' But before she could properly express her disgust he had fallen asleep again.

Mave put a blanket over him and removed the bottles from the table. He would sleep till morning. Then they would go together and see Verdun and tell him…She slipped quietly out, locking the front door behind her. Outside, dawn was beginning to lift the corner of the eastern sky.

Craig Schuster, parking his car, noted that he was the last to arrive. He had half expected Marius to be late this morning; if anyone deserved a break, he did. But there was always plenty to be done, even on the day after the festival ended. It might seem to the outsider that the fun and games, the sheer pressure of it all, was over, that everyone could take off and relax; but there was a whole new box of tricks to start on—next year's festival to be tied up, more contracts, more replacements for drop-outs. And accounting to be undertaken: it would be a long time before they knew exactly how close they had come to breaking even this year.

It was a lovely day, summer with that indefinable hint of autumn; blue skies and sparkling water were easy on the eye and senses, and the gentle breeze made for perfection. He took a long, indulgent breath. Remembering his comment to the detective, he wondered where he would be this time next year. For everything told him that it was, indeed, time to move on.

Without ties, he did not need that extra caution that the family man must have when facing an uprooting of his life. No wife to object, no children crying about a change of schools and friends. Just 'sling your hook!' Up and go when the mood came. He felt suddenly restless, a disturbing mood breaking through his hard-won calm. Probably because the police had come, first thing in the morning, to search his flat—again! And although he knew there was nothing for them to find, the reminder was unsettling.

The office air was charged with the same disturbance. Heads were down over books, ledgers, scattered papers; he nodded to one or two, but made his way silently to his own place, closing the door.

He wondered where he should go. He could wait for a job to become vacant, or take off, references in hand, and try the open market. That was perhaps the solution that most appealed. He had done well here; Marius would give him a good send-off, he was sure. Sitting at his desk, feet balanced on one corner, he felt a great sense of peace descend on him. It was always good to resolve a problem, to make some kind of definite plan to take the place of airy imagination. Refreshed, he sat up and began to work through a file of future events.

Marius put his head around the door, nodding vaguely—'Oh, there you are!'—and disappeared. For a tempting moment Craig thought he might call out to him, tell him he wanted to leave, that it was time to try a new challenge, create a new life. But he stamped down on the impulse. That was something that must be done properly, across the boss's desk, a reasoned excuse for leaving when there was still so much to do. Not as a whim, called around a closing door. He would wait for the right moment.

Coral entered and handed him a couple of letters to sign. He scribbled his signature, noting ruefully that she couldn't quite meet his eyes. Well, it would all blow over. They would all be at ease with each other, once they could put these past weeks behind them. Memories are short, and people don't like being reminded about the bad times. It would all sort itself out in due course.

25

Mave woke with a bubble of excitement somewhere in her chest. Considering how late she'd been at Hal's, the hour was ridiculously early—barely ten o'clock. She showered quickly, ate half a slice of toast and warmed yesterday's coffee, picking up the phone to call Hal. He should come with her to see Verdun. It would take him out of himself. But the phone rang several times without answer, and she replaced it. Better for him to sleep off what was probably a mammoth hangover. She would go alone into the lion's den!

Verdun was on the point of leaving his office when she arrived, and she was well aware of the veiled expression of irritation on his face. But she ignored it—he would be pleased to see her when she gave him the results of her deliberations. Even in the cold light of morning her conclusions looked promising.

'Miss Cardwell?' he said, courteously enough. 'What can I do for you?'

She grinned at him, pleased, smug. 'Perhaps it's what I can do for you, Nick!' She sat back, a magician waiting to be invited to open her magic box.

'That will make a welcome change.' He returned her grin faintly. He thought the daylight did very little for her, the heavy make-up, the irritating jangling every time she moved an arm.

'I have been thinking,' she began with some self-importance, 'about this very strange case. It seems to me so odd, knowing as I do something of the musical background, that these three fine performers should have been killed. Because there seems to be no connection.'

'I had noticed that,' he said, a trifle drily.

'Naturally! It's your job. But it worried me. I could see no point in it. It hardly seemed the work of a maniac coming in off the street.'

He stifled a sigh. 'That is true.'

'I was thinking about this last night at Hal Princeton's. He's a very sick man, you know. Killing himself! And won't go to the doctor.' She pulled herself up. 'But that's off the point. What occurred to me...' She leaned forward to make an emphasis more intensely. 'What occurred to me was that the reason we could find no connection was—because there isn't one!' She sat back triumphantly. 'There's no connection! There is *one* genuine murder, with presumably a good reason behind it, and two more to make confusion. There!' She nodded her head at him with evident satisfaction, like an old aunt unwrapping a very special gift for a favourite nephew. 'What do you think?'

Nick Verdun regarded her with a shrewd eye. He took his time answering, and she grew impatient, raising her eyebrows and nodding encouragingly. He smiled at her suddenly.

'You're a very bright lady, Mave. Have you mentioned this theory to anyone else?'

'Only to Hal last night, and he was stoned. He wouldn't remember anything.'

'Then please don't.' He hesitated. 'I believe you are right, Miss Cardwell. I have been working on that assumption for several days, ever since Mr Brammar was shot. But you should keep it to yourself. If the murderer heard that you had stumbled on his idea, you could just be in danger. I don't say you *would* be. But you might. So keep it locked away, even from Mr Princeton.'

Mave sank back in her chair. She had a distinct sense of disappointment. But Verdun, seeing her expression change, said,

'Please don't think I have anything but admiration for the way you have made your deduction. I had evidence—of a sort—while you had nothing but intuition. And I thank you for coming to me. Most people spread the good news all around them but forget about the poor struggling policeman!' He was charm itself as he stood and led her to the door. 'Remember—mum's the word.'

Despite the courtesy, she felt let down. Outside, in the balmy sunshine, she stood for a moment, wondering what was next on the agenda. The fact that Hal had not answered his phone was bothering her; not that he would thank her for caring, but she felt she needed to make certain that he was not too ill to cope with himself. She drove at something of a breakneck speed across town and drew up outside his block of flats.

He didn't answer the door, and when she tried to peer through windows they were curtained, blind eyes against the sun. Rationally, she should get on with her day's work; irrationally, she went to the janitor and asked if anyone had seen Mr Princeton this morning.

'He hasn't been round that I've seen, madam.' The man was gazing at her, intrigued. She was a sight to see in daylight.

'I'm worried about him,' she said at last. 'He's not well, you know.'

'Dead drunk, more likely,' the man said—but to himself, for this was a formidable woman. He would not like to cross her. 'I could ring him on my phone,' he suggested. She nodded.

'Good idea! You do that, and I'll go up and listen—see if there's any movement.'

She could hear the shrill phone bell. It rang a dozen times, then stopped. She called, 'Hal! Hal? Are you awake? It's Mave!'—but there was no answer. She leaned over the balcony rail to the janitor. 'Have you got a key? I think we should go in.'

He wasn't keen, she could see that. But she had a rising sense of apprehension within her, and she needed to see Hal—perhaps to order the ambulance, take the law into her own hands, make sure he had proper medical attention. It was time someone took him over, made him see sense. The force of her personality brought the keys out of the janitor's pocket, and he opened the door.

A wave of spirit-sodden air met them. Mave pulled back a curtain and looked across to the open door of the bedroom. But it wasn't necessary to search that far. The janitor was staring with dawning alarm at Hal, lying as she had left him last night, his head turned a little sideways against the chair-back, drooping towards his shoulder.

She went swiftly to him, held his arm, shook it; but even as she did instinctively the things one does under such circumstances, she knew it was too late.

'I should have stayed with him,' she said, more to herself than to the janitor. 'I should have insisted on him seeing a doctor.'

'It doesn't look as if anyone could have done much for him,' the man said. 'Seein' the way he lived an' all. Lucky to have lived this long, if you ask me.'

Mave swept to the phone. 'I didn't ask you,' she said sharply, and he shrugged, turning to the door.

'Anything you want, just ask,' he said, leaving her alone with the body of poor Hal.

Once she had called the doctor and arranged for a funeral firm to collect the body, she sat down, suddenly bereft of energy. He hadn't moved, she was sure of that. He must have sat there, lost to the world, while the life slowly drained out of him. He seemed peaceful enough, for which she was thankful; he had had little enough peace in these latter years. But it had been a shock, even though she had known, had fully realised, that he was a very sick man. At least, she reminded herself, he had gone out with the strains of his beloved Bach floating in his befuddled mind. And his review of the concert would appear today, a strange quirk of fate.

Who would write *his* obituary, she wondered? Was it failure? A failed, unsatisfied life? A waste of all the effort to be born, to grow, to learn, to comprehend? She gave a deep sigh.

'My poor old pal...how I wish I had listened to you sooner, known you better.'

The functionaries of death came and went, and Mave looked around the small flat and wondered if there was someone who should be notified, some family member long since forgotten, who might wonder from time to time what had happened to old Hal Princeton. But it was all too difficult. It had been a shock, and she needed to go out, into the sunshine, know that she was alive, that she could still feel the sun's warmth on her face, though Hal would warm to the sun no more. She closed the door behind her and went down the outside steps. The janitor was weeding the front path—probably waiting for her, she thought cynically.

'Is—was Mr Princeton paid up to date?'

'Oh, yeah. Up to the end of next month.'

'Then there's no hurry to get his stuff out?'

'No. Not if you want to keep it there.'

'We have to look for relatives, you see,' she said, less sharply. 'There may be some we don't know about.'

She drove slowly back into town, then, on an impulse, out the other side to the park. There she would find peace. There, she could sit still and think about Hal the way he deserved to be thought about—as a good friend, a sad, lonely man, a man whom life had cheated. She wanted to feel his sorrow, sense his angers. She parked the car and found a bench under a tree.

It was just one of those ridiculous coincidences that life throws at one, (evidence, she sometimes thought, of some impish god waiting to see what we will make of them), that Sir Beverly Stainer should be out walking, taking the lovely air and pondering the state of the country's balance of payments; and that he should come to her little piece of park just as she felt it was time for her to move on and tackle her work-load. She wasn't quick enough. 'Ah-ha!' he said, twiddling his fingers at her roguishly, and she sighed a deep and dreadful sigh and tried to make her getaway. But he was too much for her.

'Caught you, have I, my dear? Tut-tut! Sittin' alone on this fine mornin'? Allow me to join you.' Without waiting for her reaction (which he would have been unlikely to notice) he sat down beside her and let out a long, malodorous breath. 'And what are you doin' with yourself, m'dear?'

'Minding my own business!' sprang to mind; but she suppressed the temptation. She would be polite, distant, and then go, quickly, before he could catch up. 'Enjoying the beautiful weather, Sir Beverly.'

'Communin' with nature, eh? My stroke of luck, then!' He was too fat and repulsive to be gallant. 'Booked for lunch, are you?'

'No—yes! Well, yes, I am.' She sounded uncertain, even through the old man's hearing problem. He turned heavily to look into her face.

'Not sure, eh? Let me make up your mind for you. Lunch with me, and then a little trip on the river. You seen my little runabout?'

She had. It was a long, sleek launch, the kind one dressed up for. More Gabor than Doris Day! It would have tempted her if she could have gone alone; but she couldn't manage Sir Beverly today, not at any price, not with Hal lying dead in a morgue somewhere.

'No, thank you,' she said politely; but he wasn't one to give up. He hadn't won medals by giving up. He went into action.

'I won't take no for an answer,' he said, smirking merrily at her. 'Won't hear of it! I know what you ladies are like—you like to be persuaded!' He chuckled richly. 'Lunch first, then we'll see.'

'A sop for a good girl,' she thought. But she stood up, determined; and a lesser men, or one of greater perception, would have quailed. Sir Beverly simply laid a hot hand on her arm and squeezed it gently.

'We'll see, eh? We'll see.'

Without warning, even to herself, Mave exploded. 'We won't see! Don't you understand, you foolish man? I don't want to have lunch with you! I don't want to go in your rotten boat! I want to be left alone…'

She had surprised him, she could see that. But it took only a moment for him to recover. 'Garbo!' he said, pleased with himself. 'She said that!' He put on a heavily foreign accent. '*I want to be alo-o-one…* Well, my dear, you shall be—just as soon as we've had our lunch. We'll go on the river another day.'

Mave took a very deep breath.

'You haven't been listening, Beverly,' she said with dangerous calm. 'Go away! Leave me alone! I will not have lunch with you.' She stopped, suppressing the desire to beat him over the head. 'Do you know where I have been this morning? I have been with Hal Princeton. I have been calling the doctor, the funeral directors. I am tired and upset. Hal Princeton is dead, Beverly. Dead! And I do not wish to celebrate his death by eating lunch with you.'

At last she seemed to be making headway. He had taken the bare facts and was digesting them slowly.

'Dead, eh?' he said at last. 'Well, well, it comes to us all.' His face had drooped, a cartoon characteristic of mourning, suitable to the occasion. 'Drunk himself silly at last, has he? Well, I can't say I'm surprised. Always seemed a bit of a weakling to me. A bit of a pansy boy, if you know what I mean.'

She knew just what he meant. She had sometimes thought the same herself. But she was not going to accept it from anyone, not on this day of death, and certainly not from this great, insensitive, lumbering fool.

'He was a gentleman,' she said loudly. 'A decent, unhappy gentleman.'

The old knight got to his feet and stood squarely, legs apart, pondering on life and death, but not so as to disturb any pre-held notions.

'Sad little feller, eh? Princeton! Yankee university, you know. Princeton. Was he a Yankee, do you suppose?'

Mave turned towards him angrily. Threatened tears had evaporated in the heat of her rage, the sudden desperate warmth of her feeling for Hal. What if he *was* a 'little feller'—he was a great little feller. She wished again, with passion, that she had known, wished she had ever asked, about his own sad story. 'Oh, shut up, Beverly!' she said in tones that even he could not ignore. 'Don't be so *crass!*'

'Ass?' he said, at last taken aback by her venom. 'Oh, come on, little lady…'

'*Don't call me little lady!* Don't call me anything.' She picked up her bag and swung round on him. 'Don't even *speak* to me!'

Sir Beverly, somewhat surprised, watched her as she left, got into her car, crashed her gears and departed at speed. Women! Creatures of mood. 'She's upset,' he murmured, taking up his walk where he had left it. 'I'll speak to her when she's in a better humour.'

He took a bush path through the trees; quite chirpy again, he began to fantasise about life with Mave Cardwell. It would be stimulating, no doubt of that. She needed a firm hand. A woman appreciated knowing who was master…

He felt it had been a productive encounter—on the whole.

26

Nick Verdun stood up and stretched. He had spent the morning at his desk, going through things until he was certain he had forgotten nothing. Now he could move; and he would be as thankful as he had ever been at the end of a case that it was all over. These were decent people he had been dealing with, decent, hard-working, creative people, and he had enjoyed the contact while regretting the cause of it. Now it was all but completed. He slapped the papers together and filed them, then took his jacket from the back of his chair and went out to the car.

Marius was busy with Coral Stone when he knocked at the door; when she saw who it was she slipped tactfully away. The sight of the detective always made her acutely nervous. Marius, his hands growing sweaty, welcomed him in.

Verdun sat down and crossed his legs. 'Just one question, if you don't mind. How long ago did you finalise the arrangements with the three murder victims?'

Marius made a move towards the door to call Coral, but Verdun put up his hand. 'You find out, please.' Their eyes met, and Marius began to understand. He went to the filing cabinet. When Verdun had his answer, he left. Behind the desk, Marius sat deep in thought, trying to make proper sense of the question.

Mave reviewed a play that night; and later, try as she might, she could never remember much about it, though her review seemed to make reasonable sense. She was home by eleven-thirty, and settled down to watch a late movie. It was hard to realise that only last night she had spent hours with Hal. Now, here she was, going on with her work, living her life, and he had stopped, frozen in time. He could never catch up, she was thinking. I have to leave him there, and my last memory of him will always be of him sitting, drunk as a skunk, in his armchair.

The movie was funny, but it didn't appeal to her, and after a while she turned it off. She made herself a cup of coffee and sat down with that morning's newspaper, which for reasons beyond her control she had never got round to reading. Late night music on FM was better, and she put her feet up and tried to relax.

A knock at her door brought her heart into her mouth. She glanced at the clock: twelve-thirty. Who could possibly be calling at such an hour? She stood inside the door and called out, 'Who is it?'

'Mave!' There was urgency in the voice, and all at once she recognised it. 'Mave! Can I come in?'

She hesitated, her breath catching nervously in her throat. 'Do you know what time it is?'

'Yes. I'm sorry. I have a favour to ask of you.'

Feeling that she was probably being extremely foolish, she opened the door. He came in slowly, quiet, almost affable in his manner; but there was a disturbing undercurrent. 'Could—couldn't it have waited until tomorrow?' she said edgily.

'Forgive me. I know it seems very odd. But I need help.'

She made a decision. 'Come and sit down. Will you have some coffee?' He nodded. When she was seated opposite to him he stared down into the coffee cup and took a deep breath.

His next words surprised her. 'You're a journalist. You've got a tape recorder?'

'Yes. Why?'

'There's something I want to record. Will you do it?'

She stared at him, nonplussed. 'You've got excellent equipment down at the festival office. Why not use that?'

'This is urgent. And I don't want them to know, down there. Please?'

Suddenly he looked very tired, and Mave's heart, without warning, banged in her chest. Keeping her eyes on him, she brought the tape recorder to the table and plugged it in.

'I was sorry to hear about Hal,' he said unexpectedly. 'I know you were good friends.'

'Yes. I shall miss him.'

For a long moment neither spoke. Then Mave leaned forward and pressed the 'record' button. He ran his fingers through his hair and sat upright, his body tense.

'I wish to confess to the murders of Camille Ligorno, Piers Alessandri and Montagu Brammar.' Mave met his eyes, outwardly calm. 'I regret the necessity for committing these crimes, but I hope you will understand once you have heard me...'

It was over. Mave leaned to switch off the recorder. Her visitor sat very still, and she watched him thoughtfully, even compassionately.

'Will you tell them?' he said finally. 'And let Verdun have the tape?'

She nodded. 'What will you do?' she said at last.

'I have one more thing.'

'Not another murder?' She felt the back of her neck tingle.

'No.' He gave her a surprisingly sweet smile. 'No—not another murder.'

'Will you be all right?'

'Yes. They'll find me, of course. I know that now. I just want another couple of hours. To think.' He stood and held out his hand. 'Thank you, Mave. You've made it very easy for me.' She took the hand and held it in her own.

'But why? Why this?' She indicated the recorder, the confession.

He looked away from her. 'I thought I'd be rid of it all, once I'd completed the plan.' There was anguish in his eyes as he turned towards her. 'But it's not like that. At night...I keep seeing them...' He glanced at her, smiling quickly, full of pain. Mave put a hand out instinctively to touch his face.

'Do you have a mother?' she asked, and he looked at her oddly. 'No. She died. Some years ago.'

Mave leaned towards him. 'Then let me do what she would have done. Regardless of all that—we all need to be loved.' She kissed him on the cheek. 'Goodbye, my dear.' And before she could stop herself: 'Take care!'

He smiled at that. Then, without delay, he was gone, and she stood with the tape in her hand and had to sit down because there had been too much for one stretch of twenty-four hours, and she was no longer young and resilient.

She hardly slept. By eight-thirty she was on her way to see Verdun. His momentary alarm at seeing her changed abruptly when she put the tape cassette on his desk. 'His confession,' she said simply. 'You knew it was him, didn't you?'

He nodded. 'Yes, for the past couple of days. I thought it must be before that, but I had no proof.' He picked up the cassette. 'Where is he now?'

'He said he had one more thing to do. Not a murder,' she went on hurriedly. 'He assured me of that. But he's expecting to be picked up by you. He said he wanted another couple of hours, to think. I didn't think you'd begrudge him that.'

Verdun went to the door. His instructions were swift and urgent, and when she sat down she said, 'What are you afraid of?'

'He's unbalanced. I don't want him to kill himself.'

She hadn't thought of that possibility. 'But perhaps...' she said slowly, 'Perhaps that would be the best answer.'

'Perhaps it would. But it's not one I'm allowed to consider.' He regarded her with sympathy. 'You've had a hard time. I was sorry to hear about Mr Princeton.' She nodded, not speaking. 'I thank you for this. I'll let you know what happens.' She realised he wanted her away so that he could listen to the tape, and she stood, her face a mask of deep concern.

'Would I be able to visit him, do you think?'

'We can certainly consider that.' He escorted her to the door. 'Thank you, Miss Cardwell.'

'Mave,' she said automatically, and left him.

Verdun summoned Briggs, and when they had finished listening to the tape he sent him to ring Marius Holbein. Then he called up the men who had formed search-parties, and brought himself up to date with their progress. After which he went to his superior and gave him a full run-down on what had been happening.

'I thought this was going to be one of your unsolved cases,' said that gentleman, showing little tact.

'It's been difficult,' Verdun said without apology. 'Dealing with crims is one thing. You get to know how they think. But this was virgin ground, for all of us.'

'Got it wrapped up now, though?'

'I believe so.'

'Keep me posted.'

Marius's office was full, but no one was talking. They were waiting for Detective-Sergeant Verdun, whose call had requested a gathering at two-thirty. There was a minute to go. and they were still arriving.

No one had thought to invite Sir Beverly, and Marius had deliberately not called Dame Clarissa, preferring to tell her afterwards what had taken place. At the last moment Alicia slipped into the room and sat down beside her husband, asking questions with her eyes.

'Verdun,' he whispered, and at that moment, right on cue, the detective entered.

Without preamble he sat down at Marius's desk, his air of authority undeniable. He glanced around the room, taking in who was there, who absent, and then he smiled gravely at them.

'Thank you for giving me your time. I think you people, who have been drawn into this sad case against your wishes, have the right to know what has occurred before the media gets hold of it.' He paused, taking the tape from his pocket and fitting it into a recorder he had asked Marius to have ready. 'What I have here is the confession to three murders. It will undoubtedly be very distressing to all of you to know that it was made by one of your colleagues...'

He waited while the sudden subdued babble died away; stricken eyes glanced fearfully about the room. 'What you will hear was spoken in the presence of Miss Cardwell, who was visited late last night and was asked to do this by him.' He pressed the button. 'Anyway, judge for yourselves.'

The hiss of the tape began, and then the voice, thinned and emasculated by the machine. '*I wish to confess...*' he began; and a dreadful hush spread about the room, as if no one even wanted to breathe, lest they miss this tragic, terrible moment.

Someone, probably Gwenny, sobbed suddenly. Coral, her eyes streaming with tears, whispered, 'It's Craig!' and buried her face in her hands.

The voice ran on, sometimes smoothly, sometimes halting, as if he doubted how to express himself. '*I need to explain something that happened several years ago. At that time I was married, happily married, and we were living in America. My wife, Melanie, was deeply interested in music, and she met many visiting musicians through her work in concert promotion. We did all the things young couples do—parties, a good life-style, and we were buying our house. We hoped that in the next year or two we would be able to start a family. And one day Melanie came home full of the fact that she had met the great Piers Alessandri.*' The voice paused.

'*He was in town for longer than usual, perhaps a month, because he had been engaged by the nearby university as musician-in-residence. Our paths didn't cross socially—though I did see him at a couple of wonderful performances—because my work took me away to another state for an eight-week stint. When I came home...when I came home my wife seemed odd, quieter than usual, and I remember teasing her about becoming old and mellow. She was always such a bright, lively person...*'

The tape had clearly been switched off and then on again at this moment. '*Well, one day she broke down and told me that while I had been away she...she had...she and Alessandro had had an affair. She said she felt demeaned by it, because he had left without telling her, and clearly it had not been for him the world-shattering experience it had been for her. I told her we would try to forget it. That we had a good life ahead of us, and even though we were both badly hurt we couldn't let a man like that split us up. And I think we could have done it...'*

Coral put her hands close to her ears as if she wanted to shut out the voice, yet couldn't quite let it go.

'Then she told me,' Craig went on, dully now it seemed, *'she told me she was...'* They could hear the long, steadying breath he had taken. *'She told me that she was pregnant. I was delighted. Thrilled! But she said it was not mine—it was his. Wrong timing to be mine.'* His voice became a whisper. *'She should have kept it to herself.'*

'Oh, my God!' murmured Coral. Marius's face was pale, drawn, stiffened by withheld emotion.

'I think I decided then that something would have to be done. She was a sweet girl, innocent, it didn't occur to her to take precautions... But this feeling was a vague desire for retribution, and perhaps I would never have done anything at all. Then one day Melanie and I had a quarrel—we were both very much on edge—and she stormed out of the house...and never came back.' His voice bled tears. *'They found her in the car...over a cliff. There had been a fire...'*

Alicia took Marius's hand.

'I think I could have accepted the child. It was half Melanie's, after all, and neither of us believed in abortion. It wasn't the child's fault. But it was only a theoretical point, anyway, because I had lost them both.'

Suddenly there was strength in the voice. *'So I knew something had to be done about it. This man was a menace. He was a notorious womaniser, and now he was a murderer too. Only no one would ever convict him, he would be getting off scot free. So I had to do something!'*

Verdun was watching their faces. Jim and Mary were sitting close together, agonising over this wreckage of a marriage that, like their own approaching nuptials, had held so much promise.

'So I began to plan! I got to know someone Melanie had been friendly with in the concert promotion world, and found out where he would be for years ahead. I decided my best bet would be to settle myself in somewhere so that I would be established before he arrived. Then I would not be seen to be pursuing him. And I came to this festival, and was happy here, and almost decided to let the whole thing go. But I heard things about him, now and then, things that proved he hadn't changed. And I felt it was something I had been called to do. No one else would.'

The door opened and Clem Zacaria entered, for once subdued, not trying to hog the limelight. He stood against the doorpost and listened, and Verdun was interested to see once again that under the outrageous behaviour lurked a real man.

The voice went on. 'So, as I got to know how things operated here, I realised that it would be possible to confuse the issue, make it difficult to link the killing with me, if I chose two other people and did the same to them.'

'He's mad!' said Marius, and Alicia held his hand even tighter.

'I thought that if I chose only famous pianists, the clues would be even more difficult to follow...But I deeply regret that I had to take the lives of Madame Ligorno, such a lovely lady, and Montagu Brammar, so filled with fun. It hurt me to do it. I tried to make it as painless as I could. I waited until they had completed their work for the festival. I owed that to Marius. And they were at their peak, all of them. No decline into second-best for them...'

His voice had become dull, lifeless; still recognisable, yet not the Craig they knew.

'Madame Ligorno never really knew what was happening... She held out her hands for the flowers, and I shot her. I think she died at once. Mr Brammar went just as quickly. There was no real difficulty about either, except that I had to take my chance when I could. The first was quite easy to arrange. Mr Brammar was a little harder. I came in through the staff corridor, through the mirror door in the toilets, and hid in the cleaners' cupboard. I'd seen him talking to the policeman who was supposed to be guarding him,' (Verdun's face tightened for a moment) 'and it took only a second to slip around *the corner from the reception, into the toilets and hide. It was a near thing. I almost didn't make it. And if the copper had insisted on staying in there—but he didn't. Mr Brammar was quite insistent about it. Said he would be perfectly all right. I'd taken the chance, and it came off. Then I went out the way I'd gone in, and I waited for a moment when everyone was at sixes and sevens and re-joined the party. It was risky, but if I hadn't been able to do it then I'd have found another opportunity.'*

He sounded very tired now and went on more slowly: *'It was luck again that I happened to catch Alessandri when he was alone. I went into the recital room, and was up to the platform before he saw me. He didn't know me from Adam, of course, outside the festival. But I told him, before I shot him, that I was doing it because of Melanie. He stared. He said, "Melanie?" And then I fired. I don't believe he even remembered who Melanie was. But I felt better. I'd done what I set out to do. I believe in going straight for a goal and achieving it. And I'd done it! Then Brammar…it was a pity. He was a decent man.'*

'It is Schuster!' Clem Zacaria said. 'It is Schuster 'oo 'as done zese things?' Marius nodded, too full to speak.

'I'm sorry,' Craig was saying. *'I've caused much distress. But I'm sure you can see now that it was necessary. Men like that simply can't be allowed to walk the earth. So in that sense I don't regret it. When you find me, I hope you will remember that. I have been full of pain for so long. Thank God it's over!'* He paused. *'The gun, Mr Verdun! In the river. Leave it there. It's done its work…'*

A faint sound of distress came from the machine: Mave's recorded sadness for a tale that might have been better displayed on a theatre stage.

'Do you know where he is?' Marius said, as the detective turned the recorder off and abstracted the tape.

'No—but we've got men out everywhere. He won't get far.'

Alicia surveyed her husband's weary face. 'He doesn't mean to be caught, though, does he?'

'What do you mean?'

'He has one murder still to do—his own. You don't think this is anything but a long electronic suicide note, do you?'

Verdun overheard and nodded once. Marius turned to him 'Why did you ask me about those three engagements?'

'I wondered if it had been premeditated, or if it was a sudden piece of opportunism. The recording proves it was the former. I had already decided that was the case. When you told me that the Alessandri engagement was fairly common knowledge three years ago, even though you only signed the contracts a year later...'

'What put you on to him?'

'Partly elimination. Partly a kind of coldness about him, a holding down of emotions, I thought. He seemed as if he could do such a thing without flipping—whereas I didn't think Fletcher or Zacaria could. Then, too, he was a loner. But ultimately it was evidence, from America. We were able to tie Schuster's wife and Alessandri together. You can't have a whirlwind affair in a small community without it getting around, even if the husband's the last to know! The police over there did some poking about, and up came the dirt. So then we looked into the matter of the wife's accidental death. And, knowing what we know now, it wasn't too hard to put two and two together.'

'You think it wasn't accidental?'

'I doubt if it could be proved now. There was no proof then. A likeable couple, enjoying each other's company. Gossip! But no proof. I don't think it was accidental, myself. I'll ask him when we catch him. He has nothing to lose by being truthful about it.'

Jim, with Mary's hand in his, came forward hesitantly. 'Those phone calls?'

'Confusing the issue, I think. It meant you couldn't prove you were in the lounge at the time he hoped to be able to shoot Brammar. I get the feeling that by that time he wasn't thinking along normal lines.' He turned to Mary. 'The call to you makes little sense except to confuse us further. He's a very sick man, you know.'

Jim shuddered suddenly. 'But I might have been arrested. Didn't he care about that?'

'Put it out of your mind, sir,' Verdun urged. 'It's over.'

A policeman entered and whispered to Verdun, and he excused himself. Inside the room no one spoke. One by one they stood and wandered away, needing solitude to collect themselves. Coral dabbed her eyes with a handkerchief and went out to shut herself in the toilet.

Marius and Alicia stood by the window, staring out silently over the lovely scene as afternoon light shifted and changed. Verdun, his face grim, came to them.

'We were too late, I'm afraid.'

Alicia glanced quickly at him. 'He's killed himself!'

'Drove over the cliffs at Lachlan's Point. Much like what happened to his wife, I suppose. Perhaps he feels he'll find her again that way!'

'You're too sensitive to be a policeman,' Alicia commented, and he smiled thinly.

'That's what I sometimes tell myself!' He nodded at them and left.

27

'It's trite,' said Marius. 'But life goes on!' Alicia, knitting (a thing she normally only did on holidays), nodded sagely.

'You can get used to anything.' She was glad to see the worry lines receding from her husband's forehead. His colour was good, and he was beginning to talk productively about next year's festival. It was a good sign, even if she did wish he could switch off work for a few precious days. They were due to leave for Europe in a week or so, and then it would be a talent search for new faces to put on his stages and concert platforms and arenas. And a few museums she hadn't yet seen, she hoped.

Coral sat at Craig's desk. She hadn't wanted to, but Marius said they couldn't waste a perfectly good piece of furniture. He had appointed her acting administrative officer for the period of his absence, and she was delighted.

When she opened a drawer she found a silver pen, engraved M.S. Melanie Schuster? She held it in her hand, then pressed its cap and began to write. No good wasting a perfectly good pen. She saw no reason to hand it over to the authorities. The chapter was closed.

Sir Beverly and Dame Clarissa were taking tea together in her lounge room. The old man was holding forth about the coming budget (State, not Federal), the price of whisky, the bloody-mindedness of practically everyone he met in the course of a day. Clarissa detached her mind and followed her own thoughts, nodding and grunting when it seemed appropriate.

'Seen that woman Mave Cardwell?' he suddenly asked, and she stopped short, jolted out of her mental meanderings.

'No. Why?'

'Rather thought she fancied me at one time. Haven't seen her for days, though. Wondered if you had.'

'No. I haven't seen her. But you're wrong, you know, Beverly.'

'Wrong? How d'you make that out?'

'She doesn't fancy you!' She spoke with devastating clarity into his better ear. 'She really doesn't like you very much at all.'

Sir Beverly's face, momentarily rigid with astonishment, slowly sagged as the meaning of the words sank in. 'You sure about that, old thing?'

'Quite sure! Stop making a bloody fool of yourself, Beverly. A man of your age. Settle down to being a happy geriatric, like me.'

He sat, a wilted picture of the man he thought himself to be. 'Funny thing, Clarissa—I never thought of you as a swearing woman.'

'There are times,' she said, looking down her beaky nose at him. 'You're feeling sorry for yourself again. Come, take me for a drive.' She stood up and held out hand to him. As he struggled out of the chair she sighed. 'Greater love,' she murmured, well below his hearing range, 'has no woman! Fancy *asking* to be driven by the old fool!'

They bowled crazily along the coast road. As they passed Lachlan's Point he waved his arm, endangering several passing cyclists. 'That's where that feller drove himself off. Poor show! Police need a good blastin' for that.'

But Dame Clarissa privately thought it was all for the best.

Clem Zacaria screamed abuse at a class of leggy would-be ballerinas and flung himself into his office chair. He was thinking how strange it was that he, the volatile artiste, should never have considered for a moment killing any of the people he constantly threatened with death, while cool Craig Schuster could plan and execute three murders—and almost get away with it.

Tonight was opening night. A new ballet with a fine new star, seats well booked, show well-costumed, designed, choreographed—he had done most of it himself, so he knew it would be good.

A well-known head came round the door: Mave, looking slightly altered; but for a while he couldn't see what she had done. Then, 'You 'ave died your 'air! It is improvement.'

'I'm letting it go grey,' she corrected him. 'It was time.' She came in and sat down. 'Just came to wish you everything good for tonight.'

'You are mos' kind!' He was genuinely touched. 'You will see quality performance like you 'ave not seen before.'

'I hope it goes very well.' She hesitated. 'We're buying a wedding present for Jim Fletcher and Mary. Would you like to contribute?'

He threw back his head dramatically. 'I do not believe in marriage! It is for fools, the bourgeoisie, zose 'oo are afraid of ze conventions.'

Mave sighed and levered herself out of the ugly chair, pausing to survey him thoughtfully. There was a lonely, solitary look about him; the fine bones and spare figure were still boyish. But there was, too, an indefinable tragedy in the dark eyes, and she gave him a swift, almost predatory smile.

'We must have lunch together some time!'

For a moment he did not comprehend. Then a flicker of fear broke through the tragic expression, and his hands came out to ward her off. He had, she thought (almost with affection), something of that quality of desolation that had drawn her to Hal.

'Well—in the theatre they say "break a leg" before a first night. I don't know what they say in ballet.' She gave him a little wave as she disappeared through the doorway. 'Break a leg, Zacaria!'

And that night, in full view of a capacity audience, he did.

THE END